The

Making

of a

Marchioness

Watchmaker Publishing

1931

Emily Fox-Seton

EMILY FOX-SETON

BEING "THE MAKING OF A MARCHIONESS"

By

Frances Hodgson Burnett

Illustrated By C.D. Williams

S R

Copyright © 2010 Watchmaker PUB

ISBN 978-1-60386-359-9

Chapter
One

When Miss Fox-Seton descended from the
twopenny bus as it drew up, she
gathered her trim tailor-made skirt about
her with neatness and decorum, being well used to
getting in and out of twopenny buses and to making
her way across muddy London streets. A woman
whose tailor-made suit must last two or three years
soon learns how to protect it from splashes, and how
to aid it to retain the freshness of its folds. During her
trudging about this morning in the wet, Emily Fox-
Seton had been very careful, and, in fact, was
returning to Mortimer Street as unspotted as she had
left it. She had been thinking a good deal about her
dress—this particular faithful one which she had
already worn through a twelvemonth. Skirts had
made one of their appalling changes, and as she
walked down Regent Street and Bond Street she had
stopped at the windows of more than one shop
bearing the sign "Ladies' Tailor and Habit-Maker," and
had looked at the tautly attired, preternaturally slim

models, her large, honest hazel eyes wearing an anxious expression. She was trying to discover *where* seams were to be placed and how gathers were to be hung; or if there were to be gathers at all; or if one had to be bereft of every seam in a style so unrelenting as to forbid the possibility of the honest and semi-penniless struggling with the problem of remodeling last season's skirt at all. "As it is only quite an ordinary brown," she had murmured to herself, "I might be able to buy a yard or so to match it, and I *might* be able to join the gore near the pleats at the back so that it would not be seen."

She quite beamed as she reached the happy conclusion. She was such a simple, normal-minded creature that it took but little to brighten the aspect of life for her and to cause her to break into her good-natured, childlike smile. A little kindness from any one, a little pleasure or a little comfort, made her glow with nice-tempered enjoyment. As she got out of the bus, and picked up her rough brown skirt, prepared to tramp bravely through the mud of Mortimer Street to her lodgings, she was positively radiant. It was not only her smile which was childlike, her face itself was childlike for a woman of her age and size. She was thirty-four and a well-set-up creature, with fine square shoulders and a long small waist and good hips. She was a big woman, but carried herself well, and having solved the problem of obtaining, through marvels of energy and management, one good dress a year, wore it so well, and changed her old ones so dexterously, that she always looked rather smartly dressed. She had nice, round, fresh cheeks and nice, big, honest eyes, plenty of mouse-brown hair and a short, straight nose. She was striking and well-bred-looking, and her plenitude of good-natured interest in everybody, and her pleasure in everything out of which pleasure could be wrested, gave her big eyes a fresh look which made her seem rather like a nice overgrown girl than a mature woman whose life was a continuous struggle with the narrowest of mean fortunes.

She was a woman of good blood and of good education, as the education of such women goes. She had few relatives, and none of them had any intention of burdening themselves with her pennilessness. They were people of excellent family, but had quite enough to do to keep their sons in the army or navy and find husbands for their daughters. When Emily's mother had died and her small annuity had died with her, none of them had wanted the care of a big raw-boned girl, and Emily had had the situation frankly explained to her. At eighteen she had begun to work as assistant teacher in a small school; the year following she had taken a place as nursery-governess; then she had been reading-companion to an unpleasant old woman in Northumberland. The old woman had lived in the country, and her relatives had hovered over her like vultures awaiting her decease. The household had been gloomy and gruesome enough to have driven into melancholy madness any girl not of the sanest and most matter-of-fact temperament. Emily Fox-Seton had endured it with an unfailing good nature, which at last had actually awakened in the breast of her mistress a ray of human feeling. When the old woman at length died, and Emily was to be turned out into the world, it was revealed that she had been left a legacy of a few hundred pounds, and a letter containing some rather practical, if harshly expressed, advice.

Go back to London [Mrs. Maytham had written in her feeble, crabbed hand]. You are not clever enough to do anything remarkable in the way of earning your living, but you are so good-natured that you can make yourself useful to a lot of helpless creatures who will pay you a trifle for looking after them and the affairs they are too lazy or too foolish to manage for themselves. You might get on to one of the second-class fashion-papers to answer ridiculous questions about house-keeping or wall-papers or freckles. You know the kind of thing I mean. You might write notes or do accounts and shopping for some lazy woman. You are a practical, honest creature, and you have good manners. I have often thought that you had just the kind of commonplace gifts that a host of commonplace people want to find at their service. An old servant of mine who lives in Mortimer Street would probably give you cheap, decent lodgings, and behave well to you for my sake. She has reason to be fond of me. Tell her I sent you to her, and that she must take you in for ten shillings a week.

Emily wept for gratitude, and ever afterward enthroned old Mrs. Maytham on an altar as a princely and sainted benefactor, though after she had invested her legacy she got only twenty pounds a year from it.

"It was so *kind* of her," she used to say with heartfelt humbleness of spirit. "I never *dreamed* of her doing such a generous thing. I hadn't a *shadow* of a claim upon her—not a *shadow*." It was her way to express her honest emotions with emphasis which italicised, as it were, her outpourings of pleasure or appreciation.

She returned to London and presented herself to the ex-serving-woman. Mrs. Cupp had indeed reason to remember her mistress gratefully. At a time when youth and indiscreet affection had betrayed her disastrously, she had been saved from open disgrace and taken care of by Mrs. Maytham.

The old lady, who had then been a vigorous, sharp-tongued, middle-aged woman, had made the soldier lover marry his despairing sweetheart, and when he had promptly drunk himself to death, she had set her up in a lodging-house which had thriven and enabled her to support herself and her daughter decently.

In the second story of her respectable, dingy house there was a small room which she went to some trouble to furnish up for her dead mistress's friend. It was made into a bed-sitting-room with the aid of a cot which Emily herself bought and disguised decently as a couch during the daytime, by means of a red and blue Como blanket. The one window of the room looked out upon a black little back-yard and a sooty wall on which thin cats crept stealthily or sat and mournfully gazed at fate. The Como rug played a large part in the decoration of the apartment. One of them, with a piece of tape run through a hem, hung over the door in the character of a *portière*; another covered a corner which was Miss Fox-Seton's sole wardrobe. As she began to get work, the cheerful, aspiring creature bought herself a Kensington carpet-square, as red as Kensington art would permit it to be. She covered her chairs with Turkey-red cotton, frilling them round the seats. Over her cheap white muslin curtains (eight and eleven a pair at Robson's) she hung Turkey-red draperies. She bought a cheap cushion at one of Liberty's sales, and some bits of twopenny-halfpenny art china for her narrow mantelpiece. A lacquered tea-tray and a tea-set of a single cup and saucer, a plate and a teapot, made her feel herself almost sumptuous. After a day spent in trudging about in the wet or cold of the streets, doing other people's shopping, or searching for dressmakers or servants' characters for her patrons, she used to think of her bed-sitting-room with joyful anticipation. Mrs. Cupp always had a bright fire glowing in her tiny grate when she came in, and when her lamp was lighted under its home-made shade of crimson Japanese paper, its cheerful air, combining itself with the singing of her little, fat, black kettle on the hob, seemed absolute luxury to a tired, damp woman.

Mrs. Cupp and Jane Cupp were very kind and attentive to her. No one who lived in the same house with her could have helped liking her. She gave so little trouble, and was so expansively pleased by any attention, that the Cupps,—who were sometimes rather bullied and snubbed by the "professionals" who generally occupied their other rooms,—quite loved her. Sometimes the "professionals," extremely smart ladies and gentlemen who did turns at the balls or played small parts at theatres, were irregular in their payments or went away leaving bills behind them; but Miss Fox-Seton's payments were as regular as Saturday night, and, in fact, there had been times when, luck being against her, Emily had gone extremely hungry during a whole week rather than buy her lunches at the ladies' tea-shops with the money that would pay her rent.

In the honest minds of the Cupps, she had become a sort of possession of which they were proud. She seemed to bring into their dingy lodging-house a touch of the great world,—that world whose people lived in Mayfair and had country-houses where they entertained parties for the shooting and the hunting, and in which also existed the maids and matrons who on cold spring mornings sat, amid billows of satin and tulle and lace, surrounded with nodding plumes, waiting, shivering, for hours in their carriages that they might at last enter Buckingham Palace and be admitted to the Drawing-room. Mrs. Cupp knew that Miss Fox-Seton was "well connected;" she knew that she possessed an aunt with a title, though her ladyship never took the slightest notice of her niece. Jane Cupp took "Modern Society," and now and then had the pleasure of reading aloud to her young man little incidents concerning some castle or manor in which Miss Fox-Seton's aunt, Lady Malfry, was staying with earls and special favorites of the Prince's. Jane also knew that Miss Fox-Seton occasionally sent letters addressed "To the Right Honourable the Countess of So-and-so," and received replies stamped with coronets. Once even a letter had arrived adorned with strawberry-leaves, an incident which Mrs. Cupp and Jane had discussed with deep interest over their hot buttered-toast and tea.

Emily Fox-Seton, however, was far from making any professions of grandeur. As time went on she had become fond enough of the Cupps to be quite frank with them about her connections with these grand people. The countess had heard from a friend that Miss Fox-Seton had once found her an excellent governess, and she had commissioned her to find for her a reliable young ladies' serving-maid. She had done some secretarial work for a charity of which the duchess was patroness. In fact, these people knew her only as a well-bred woman who for a modest remuneration would make herself extremely useful in numberless practical ways. She knew much more of them than they knew of her, and, in her affectionate admiration for those who treated her with human kindness, sometimes spoke to Mrs. Cupp or Jane of their beauty or charity with a very nice, ingenuous feeling. Naturally some of her patrons grew fond of her, and as she was a fine, handsome young woman with a perfectly correct bearing, they gave her little pleasures, inviting her to tea or luncheon, or taking her to the theatre.

Her enjoyment of these things was so frank and grateful that the Cupps counted them among their own joys. Jane Cupp—who knew something of dressmaking—felt it a brilliant thing to be called upon to renovate an old dress or help in the making of a new one for some festivity. The Cupps thought their tall, well-built lodger something of a beauty, and when they had helped her to dress for the evening, baring her fine, big white neck and arms, and adorning her thick braids of hair with some sparkling, trembling ornaments, after putting her in her four-wheeled cab, they used to go back to their kitchen and talk about her, and wonder that some gentleman who wanted a handsome, stylish woman at the head of his table, did not lay himself and his fortune at her feet.

"In the photograph-shops in Regent Street you see many a lady in a coronet that hasn't half the good looks she has," Mrs. Cupp remarked frequently. "She's got a nice complexion and a fine head of hair, and—if you ask *me*—she's got as nice a pair of clear eyes as a lady could have. Then look at her figure—her neck and her waist! That kind of big long throat of hers would set off rows of pearls or diamonds beautiful! She's a lady born, too, for all her simple, every-day way; and she's a sweet creature, if ever there was one. For kind-heartedness and good-nature I never saw her equal."

Miss Fox-Seton had middle-class patrons as well as noble ones,—in fact, those of the middle class were far more numerous than the duchesses,—so it had been possible for her to do more than one good turn for the Cupp household. She had got sewing in Maida Vale and Bloomsbury for Jane Cupp many a time, and Mrs. Cupp's dining-room floor had been occupied for years by a young man Emily had been able to recommend. Her own appreciation of good turns made her eager to do them for others. She never let slip a chance to help anyone in any way.

It was a good-natured thing done by one of her patrons who liked her, which made her so radiant as she walked through the mud this morning. She was inordinately fond of the country, and having had what she called "a bad winter," she had not seen the remotest chance of getting out of town at all during the summer months. The weather was beginning to be unusually hot, and her small red room, which seemed so cosy in winter, was shut in by a high wall from all chance of breezes. Occasionally she lay and panted a little in her cot, and felt that when all the private omnibuses, loaded with trunks and servants, had rattled away and deposited their burdens at the various stations, life in town would be rather lonely. Every one she knew would have gone somewhere, and Mortimer Street in August was a melancholy thing.

And Lady Maria had actually invited her to Mallowe. What a piece of good fortune-what an extraordinary piece of kindness!

She did not know what a source of entertainment she was to Lady Maria, and how the shrewd, worldly old thing liked her. Lady Maria Bayne was the cleverest, sharpest-tongued, smartest old woman in London. She knew everybody and had done everything in her youth, a good many things not considered highly proper. A certain royal duke had been much pleased with her and people had said some very nasty things about it. But this had not hurt Lady Maria. She knew how to say nasty things herself, and as she said them wittily they were usually listened to and repeated.

Emily Fox-Seton had gone to her first to write notes for an hour every evening. She had sent, declined, and accepted invitations, and put off charities and dull people. She wrote a fine, dashing hand, and had a matter-of-fact intelligence and knowledge of things. Lady Maria began to depend on her and to find that she could be sent on errands and depended on to do a number of things. Consequently, she was often at South Audley Street, and once, when Lady Maria was suddenly taken ill and was horribly frightened about herself, Emily was such a comfort to her that she kept her for three weeks.

"The creature is so cheerful and perfectly free from vice that she's a relief," her ladyship said to her nephew afterward. "So many women are affected cats. She'll go out and buy you a box of pills or a porous plaster, but at the same time she has a kind of simplicity and freedom from spites and envies which might be the natural thing for a princess."

So it happened that occasionally Emily put on her best dress and most carefully built hat and went to South Audley Street to tea. (Sometimes she had previously gone in buses to some remote place in the City to buy a special tea of which there had been rumours.) She met some very smart people and rarely any stupid ones, Lady Maria being incased in a perfect, frank armour of good-humoured selfishness, which would have been capable of burning dulness at the stake.

"I won't have dull people," she used to say. "I'm dull myself."

When Emily Fox-Seton went to her on the morning in which this story opens, she found her consulting her visiting-book and making lists.

"I'm arranging my parties for Mallowe," she said rather crossly. "How tiresome it is! The people one wants at the same time are always nailed to the opposite ends of the earth. And then things are found out about people, and one can't have them till it's blown over. Those ridiculous Dexters! They were the nicest possible pair—both of them good-looking and both of them ready to flirt with anybody. But there was too much flirting, I suppose. Good heavens! if I couldn't have a scandal and keep it quiet, I wouldn't have a scandal at all. Come and help me, Emily."

Emily sat down beside her.

"You see, it is my early August party," said her ladyship, rubbing her delicate little old nose with her pencil, "and Walderhurst is coming to me. It always amuses me to have Walderhurst. The moment a man like that comes into a room the women begin to frisk about and swim and languish, except those who try to get up interesting conversations they think likely to attract his attention. They all think it is possible that he may marry them. If he were a Mormon he might have marchionesses of Walderhurst of all shapes and sizes."

"I suppose," said Emily, "that he was very much in love with his first wife and will never marry again."

"He wasn't in love with her any more than he was in love with his housemaid. He knew he must marry, and thought it very annoying. As the child died, I believe he thinks it his duty to marry again. But he hates it. He's rather dull, and he can't bear women fussing about and wanting to be made love to."

They went over the visiting-book and discussed people and dates seriously. The list was made and the notes written before Emily left the house. It was not until she had got up and was buttoning her coat that Lady Maria bestowed her boon.

"Emily," she said, "I am going to ask you to Mallowe on the 2d. I want you to help me to take care of people and keep them from boring me and one another, though I don't mind their boring one another half so much as I mind their boring me. I want to be able to go off and take my nap at any hour I choose. I will *not* entertain people. What you can do is to lead them off to gather things of look at church towers. I hope you'll come."

Emily Fox-Seton's face flushed rosily, and her eyes opened and sparkled.

"O Lady Maria, you *are* kind!" she said. "You know how I should enjoy it. I have heard so much of Mallowe. Everyone says it is so beautiful and that there are no such gardens in England."

"They are good gardens. My husband was rather mad about roses. The best train for you to take is the 2:30 from Paddington. That will bring you to the Court just in time for tea on the lawn."

Emily could have kissed Lady Maria if they had been on the terms which lead people to make demonstrations of affection. But she would have been quite as likely to kiss the butler when he bent over her at dinner and murmured in dignified confidence, "Port or sherry, miss?" Bibsworth would have been no more astonished than Lady Maria would, and Bibsworth certainly would have expired of disgust and horror.

She was so happy when she hailed the twopenny bus that when she got into it her face was beaming with the delight which adds freshness and good looks to any woman. To think that such good luck had come to her! To think of leaving her hot little room behind her and going as a guest to one of the most beautiful old houses in England! How delightful it would be to live for a while quite naturally the life the fortunate people lived year after year—to be a part of the beautiful order and picturesqueness and dignity of it! To sleep in a lovely bedroom, to be called in the morning by a perfect housemaid, to have one's early tea served in a delicate cup, and to listen as one drank it to the birds singing in the trees in the park! She had an ingenuous appreciation of the simplest material joys, and the fact that she would wear her nicest clothes every day, and dress for dinner every evening, was a delightful thing to reflect upon. She got so much more out of life than most people, though she was not aware of it.

She opened the front door of the house in Mortimer Street with her latch-key, and went upstairs, almost unconscious that the damp heat was dreadful. She met Jane Cupp coming down, and smiled at her happily.

"Jane," she said, "if you are not busy, I should like to have a little talk with you. Will you come into my room?"

"Yes, miss," Jane replied, with her usual respectful lady's maid's air. It was in truth Jane's highest ambition to become someday maid to a great lady, and she privately felt that her association with Miss Fox-Seton was the best possible training. She used to ask to be allowed to dress her when she went out, and had felt it a privilege to be permitted to "do" her hair.

She helped Emily to remove her walking dress, and neatly folded away her gloves and veil. She knelt down before her as soon as she saw her seat herself to take off her muddy boots.

"Oh, *thank* you, Jane," Emily exclaimed, with her kind italicised manner. "That *is* good of you. I *am* tired, really. But such a nice thing has happened. I have had such a delightful invitation for the first week in August."

"I'm sure you'll enjoy it, miss," said Jane. "It's so hot in August."

"Lady Maria Bayne has been kind enough to invite me to Mallowe Court," explained Emily, smiling down at the cheap slipper Jane was putting on her large, well-shaped foot. She was built on a large scale, and her foot was of no Cinderella-like proportions.

"O miss!" exclaimed Jane. "How beautiful! I was reading about Mallowe in 'Modern Society' the other day, and it said it was lovely and her ladyship's parties were wonderful for smartness. The paragraph was about the Marquis of Walderhurst."

"He is Lady Maria's cousin," said Emily, "and he will be there when I am."

She was a friendly creature, and lived a life so really isolated from any ordinary companionship that her simple little talks with Jane and Mrs. Cupp were a pleasure to her. The Cupps were neither gossiping nor intrusive, and she felt as if they were her friends. Once when she had been ill for a week she remembered suddenly realising that she had no intimates at all, and that if she died Mrs. Cupp's and Jane's would certainly be the last faces—and the only ones—she would see. She had cried a little the night she thought of it, but then, as she told herself, she was feverish and weak, and it made her morbid.

"It was because of this invitation that I wanted to talk to you, Jane," she went on. "You see, we shall have to begin to contrive about dresses."

"Yes, indeed, miss. It's fortunate that the summer sales are on, isn't it? I saw some beautiful colored linens yesterday. They were so cheap, and they do make up so smart for the country. Then you've got your new Tussore with the blue collar and waistband. It does become you."

"I must say I think that a Tussore always looks fresh," said Emily, "and I saw a really nice little tan toque—one of those soft straw ones—for three and eleven. And just a twist of blue chiffon and a wing would make it look quite *good*."

She was very clever with her fingers, and often did excellent things with a bit of chiffon and a wing, or a few yards of linen or muslin and a remnant of lace picked up at a sale. She and Jane spent quite a happy afternoon in careful united contemplation of the resources of her limited wardrobe. They found that the brown skirt *could* be altered, and, with the addition of new *revers* and collar and a *jabot* of string-coloured lace at the neck, would look quite fresh. A black net evening dress, which a patron had good-naturedly given her the year before, could be remodeled and touched up delightfully. Her fresh face and her square white shoulders were particularly adorned by black. There was a white dress which could be sent to the cleaner's, and an old pink one whose superfluous breadths could be combined with lace and achieve wonders.

"Indeed, I think I shall be very well off for dinner-dresses," said Emily. "Nobody expects me to change often. Everyone knows—if they notice at all." She did not know she was humble-minded and of an angelic contentedness of spirit. In fact, she did not find herself interested in contemplation of her own qualities, but in contemplation and admiration of those of other people. It was necessary to provide Emily Fox-Seton with food and lodging and such a wardrobe as would be just sufficient credit to her more fortunate acquaintances. She worked hard to attain this modest end and was quite satisfied. She found at the shops where the summer sales were being held a couple of cotton frocks to which her height and her small, long waist gave an air of actual elegance. A sailor hat, with a smart ribbon and well-set quill, a few new trifles for her neck, a bow, a silk handkerchief daringly knotted, and some fresh gloves, made her feel that she was sufficiently equipped.

During her last expedition to the sales she came upon a nice white duck coat and skirt which she contrived to buy as a present for Jane. It was necessary to count over the contents of her purse very carefully and to give up the purchase of a slim umbrella she wanted, but she did it cheerfully. If she had been a rich woman she would have given presents to everyone she knew, and it was actually a luxury to her to be able to do something for the Cupps, who, she always felt, were continually giving her more than she paid for. The care they took of her small room, the fresh hot tea they managed to have ready when she came in, the penny bunch of daffodils they sometimes put on her table, were kindnesses, and she was grateful for them. "I am very much obliged to you, Jane," she said to the girl, when she got into the four-wheeled cab on the eventful day of her journey to Mallowe. "I don't know what I should have done without you, I'm sure. I feel so smart in my dress now that you have altered it. If Lady Maria's maid ever thinks of leaving her, I am sure I could recommend you for her place."

Chapter
Two

There were other visitors to Mallowe Court
travelling by the 2:30 from Paddington, but
they were much smarter people than Miss
Fox-Seton, and they were put into a first-class
carriage by a footman with a cockade and a long
drab coat. Emily, who traveled third with some
workmen with bundles, looked out of her window as
they passed, and might possibly have breathed a faint
sigh if she had not felt in such buoyant spirits. She
had put on her revived brown skirt and a white linen
blouse with a brown dot on it. A soft brown silk tie
was knotted smartly under her fresh collar, and she
wore her new sailor hat. Her gloves were brown, and
so was her parasol. She looked nice and taut and
fresh, but notably inexpensive. The people who went
to sales and bought things at three and eleven or
"four-three" a yard would have been able add her up
and work out her total. But there would be no
people capable of the calculation at Mallowe. Even
the servants' hall was likely to know less of prices

than this one guest did. The people the drab-coated footman escorted to the first-class carriage were a mother and daughter. The mother had regular little features, and would have been pretty if she had not been much too plump. She wore an extremely smart travelling-dress and a wonderful dust-cloak of cool, pale, thin silk. She was not an elegant person, but her appointments were luxurious and self-indulgent. Her daughter was pretty, and had a slim, swaying waist, soft pink cheeks, and a pouting mouth. Her large picture-hat of pale-blue straw, with its big gauze bow and crushed roses, had a slightly exaggerated Parisian air.

"It is a little too picturesque," Emily thought; "but how lovely she looks in it! I suppose it was so becoming she could not help buying it. I'm sure it's Virot."

As she was looking at the girl admiringly, a man passed her window. He was a tall man with a square face. As he passed close to Emily, he stared through her head as if she had been transparent or invisible. He got into the smoking-carriage next to her.

When the train arrived at Mallowe station, he was one of the first persons who got out. Two of Lady Maria's men were waiting on the platform. Emily recognised their liveries. One met the tall man, touching his hat, and followed him to a high cart, in the shafts of which a splendid iron-gray mare was fretting and dancing. In a few moments the arrival was on the high seat, the footman behind, and the mare speeding up the road. Miss Fox-Seton found herself following the second footman and the mother and daughter, who were being taken to the landau waiting outside the station. The footman piloted them, merely touching his hat quickly to Emily, being fully aware that she could take care of herself.

This she did promptly, looking after her box, and seeing it safe in the Mallowe omnibus. When she reached the landau, the two other visitors were in it. She got in, and in entire contentment sat down with her back to the horses.

The mother and daughter wore for a few minutes a somewhat uneasy air. They were evidently sociable persons, but were not quite sure how to begin a conversation with an as yet unintroduced lady who was going to stay at the country house to which they were themselves invited.

Emily herself solved the problem, producing her commonplace with a friendly tentative smile.

"Isn't it a lovely country?" she said.

"It's perfect," answered the mother. "I've never visited Europe before, and the English country seems to me just exquisite. We have a summer place in America, but the country is quite different."

She was good-natured and disposed to talk, and, with Emily Fox-Seton's genial assistance, conversation flowed. Before they were half-way to Mallowe, it had revealed itself that they were from Cincinnati, and after a winter spent in Paris, largely devoted to visits to Paquin, Doucet, and Virot, they had taken a house in Mayfair for the season. Their name was Brooke. Emily thought she remembered hearing of them as people who spent a great deal of money and went incessantly to parties, always in new and lovely clothes. The girl had been presented by the American minister, and had had a sort of success because she dressed and danced exquisitely. She was the kind of

American girl who ended by marrying a title. She had sparkling eyes and a delicate tip-tilted nose. But even Emily guessed that she was an astute little person.

"Have you ever been to Mallowe Court before?" she inquired.

"No; and I am *so* looking forward to it. It is so beautiful."

"Do you know Lady Maria very well?"

"I've known her about three years. She has been very kind to me."

"Well, I shouldn't have taken her for a particularly kind person. She's too sharp."

Emily amiably smiled. "She's so clever," she replied.

"Do you know the Marquis of Walderhurst?" asked Mrs. Brooke.

"No," answered Miss Fox-Seton. She had no part in that portion of Lady Maria's life which was illumined by cousins who were marquises. Lord Walderhurst did not drop in to afternoon tea. He kept himself for special dinner-parties.

"Did you see the man who drove away in the high cart?" Mrs. Brooke continued, with a touch of fevered interest. "Cora thought it must be the marquis. The servant who met him wore the same livery as the man up there"—with a nod toward the box.

"It was one of Lady Maria's servants," said Emily; "I have seen him in South Audley Street. And Lord Walderhurst was to be at Mallowe. Lady Maria mentioned it."

"There, mother!" exclaimed Cora.

"Well, of course if he is to be there, it will make it interesting," returned her mother, in a tone in which lurked an admission of relief. Emily wondered if she had wanted to go somewhere else and had been firmly directed toward Mallowe by her daughter.

"We heard a great deal of him in London this season," Mrs. Brooks went on.

Miss Cora Brooke laughed.

"We heard that at least half a dozen people were determined to marry him," she remarked with pretty scorn. "I should think that to meet a girl who was indifferent might be good for him."

"Don't be too indifferent, Cora," said her mother, with ingenuous ineptness.

It was a very stupid bit of revelation, and Miss Brooke's eyes flashed. If Emily Fox-Seton had been a sharp woman, she would have observed that, if the *rôle* of indifferent and piquant young person could be made dangerous to Lord Walderhurst, it would be made so during this visit. The man was in peril from this beauty from Cincinnati and her rather indiscreet mother, though upon the whole, the indiscreet maternal parent might unconsciously form his protection.

But Emily only laughed amiably, as at a humorous remark. She was ready to accept almost anything as humour.

"Well, he *would* be a great match for any girl," she said. "He is so rich, you know. He is very rich."

When they reached Mallowe, and were led out upon the lawn, where the tea was being served under embowering trees, they found a group of guests eating little hot cakes and holding teacups in their hands. There were several young women, and one of them—a very tall, very fair girl, with large eyes as blue as forget-me-nots, and with a lovely, limp, and long blue frock of the same shade—had been one of the beauties of the past season. She was a Lady Agatha Slade, and Emily began to admire her at once. She felt her to be a sort of added boon bestowed by kind Fate upon herself. It was so delightful that she should be of this particular house-party—this lovely creature, whom she had only known previously through pictures in ladies' illustrated papers. If it should occur to her to wish to become the Marchioness of Walderhurst, what could possibly prevent the consummation of her desire? Surely not Lord Walderhurst himself, if he was human. She was standing, leaning lightly against the trunk of an ilex-tree, and a snow-white Borzoi was standing close to her, resting his long, delicate head against her gown, encouraging the caresses of her fair, stroking hand. She was in this attractive pose when Lady Maria turned in her seat and said:

"There's Walderhurst."

The man who had driven himself over from the station in the cart was coming towards them across the grass. He was past middle life and plain, but was of good height and had an air. It was perhaps, on the whole, rather an air of knowing what he wanted.

Emily Fox-Seton, who by that time was comfortably seated in a cushioned basket-chair, sipping her own cup of tea, gave him the benefit of the doubt when she wondered if he was not really distinguished and aristocratic-looking. He was really neither, but was well-built and well-dressed, and had good grayish-brown eyes, about the colour of his grayish-brown hair. Among these amiably worldly people, who were not in the least moved by an altruistic prompting, Emily's greatest capital consisted in the fact that she did not expect to be taken the least notice of. She was not aware that it was her capital, because the fact was so wholly a part of the simple contentedness of her nature that she had not thought about it at all. The truth was that she found all her entertainment and occupation in being an audience or a spectator. It did not occur to her to notice that, when the guests were presented to him, Lord Walderhurst barely glanced at her surface as he bowed, and could scarcely be said to forget her existence the next second, because he had hardly gone to the length of recognising it. As she enjoyed her extremely nice cup of tea and little buttered scone, she also enjoyed looking at his Lordship discreetly, and trying to make an innocent summing up of his mental attitudes.

Lady Maria seemed to like him and to be pleased to see him. He himself seemed, in an undemonstrative way, to like Lady Maria. He also was evidently glad to get his tea, and enjoyed it as he sat at his cousin's side. He did not pay very much attention to anyone else. Emily was slightly disappointed to see that he did not glance at the beauty and the Borzoi more than twice, and then that his examination seemed as much for the Borzoi as for the beauty. She could not help also observing that since he had joined the circle it had become more animated, so far at least as the female members were concerned. She could not help remembering Lady

Maria's remark about the effect he produced on women when he entered a room. Several interesting or sparkling speeches had already been made. There was a little more laughter and chattiness, which somehow it seemed to be quite open to Lord Walderhurst to enjoy, though it was not exactly addressed to him. Miss Cora Brooke, however, devoted herself to a young man in white flannels with an air of tennis about him. She sat a little apart and talked to him in a voice soft enough to even exclude Lord Walderhurst. Presently she and her companion got up and sauntered away. They went down the broad flight of ancient stone steps which led to the tennis-court, lying in full view below the lawn. There they began to play tennis. Miss Brooke skimmed and darted about like a swallow. The swirl of her lace petticoats was most attractive.

"That girl ought not to play tennis in shoes with ridiculous heels," remarked Lord Walderhurst. "She will spoil the court."

Lady Maria broke into a little chuckle.

"She wanted to play at this particular moment," she said. "And as she has only just arrived, it did not occur to her to come out to tea in tennis-shoes."

"She'll spoil the court all the same," said the marquis. "What clothes! It's amazing how girls dress now."

"I wish I had such clothes," answered Lady Maria, and she chuckled again. "She's got beautiful feet."

"She's got Louis Quinze heels," returned his Lordship.

At all events, Emily Fox-Seton thought Miss Brooke seemed to intend to rather keep out of his way and to practise no delicate allurements. When her tennis-playing was at an end, she sauntered about the lawn and terraces with her companion, tilting her parasol prettily over her shoulder, so that it formed an entrancing background to her face and head. She seemed to be entertaining the young man. His big laugh and the silver music of her own lighter merriment rang out a little tantalisingly.

"I wonder what Cora is saying," said Mrs. Brooke to the group at large. "She always makes men laugh so."

Emily Fox-Seton felt an interest herself, the merriment sounded so attractive. She wondered if perhaps to a man who had been so much run after a girl who took no notice of his presence and amused other men so much might not assume an agreeable aspect.

But he took more notice of Lady Agatha Slade than of anyone else that evening. She was placed next to him at dinner, and she really was radiant to look upon in palest green chiffon. She had an exquisite little head, with soft hair piled with wondrous lightness upon it, and her long little neck swayed like the stem of a flower. She was lovely enough to arouse in the beholder's mind the anticipation of her being silly, but she was not silly at all.

Lady Maria commented upon that fact to Miss Fox-Seton when they met in her bedroom late that night. Lady Maria liked to talk and be talked to for half an hour after the day was over, and Emily Fox-Seton's admiring interest in all she said she found at once stimulating and soothing. Her Ladyship was an old woman who indulged and inspired herself with an Epicurean wisdom. Though she would not have stupid people about her, she did not always want very clever ones.

"They give me too much exercise," she said. "The epigrammatic ones keep me always jumping over fences. Besides, I like to make all the epigrams myself."

Emily Fox-Seton struck a happy mean, and she was a genuine admirer. She was intelligent enough not to spoil the point of an epigram when she repeated it, and she might be relied upon to repeat it and give all the glory to its originator. Lady Maria knew there were people who, hearing your good things, appropriated them without a scruple. To-night she said a number of good things to Emily in summing up her guests and their characteristics.

"Walderhurst has been to me three times when I made sure that he would not escape without a new marchioness attached to him. I should think he would take one to put an end to the annoyance of dangling unplucked upon the bough. A man in his position, if he has character enough to choose, can prevent even his wife's being a nuisance. He can give her a good house, hang the family diamonds on her, supply a decent elderly woman as a sort of lady-in-waiting and turn her into the paddock to kick up her heels within the limits of decorum. His own rooms can be sacred to him. He has his clubs and his personal interests. Husbands and wives annoy each other very little in these days. Married life has become comparatively decent."

"I should think his wife might be very happy," commented Emily. "He looks very kind."

"I don't know whether he is kind or not. It has never been necessary for me to borrow money from him."

Lady Maria was capable of saying odd things in her refined little drawling voice.

"He's more respectable than most men of his age. The diamonds are magnificent, and he not only has three superb places, but has money enough to keep them up. Now, there are three aspirants at Mallowe in the present party. Of course you can guess who they are, Emily?"

Emily Fox-Seton almost blushed. She felt a little indelicate.

"Lady Agatha would be very suitable," she said. "And Mrs. Ralph is very clever, of course. And Miss Brooke is really pretty."

Lady Maria gave vent to her small chuckle.

"Mrs. Ralph is the kind of woman who means business. She'll corner Walderhurst and talk literature and roll her eyes at him until he hates her. These writing women, who are intensely pleased with themselves, if they have some good looks into the bargain, believe themselves capable of marrying any one. Mrs. Ralph has fine eyes and rolls them. Walderhurst won't be ogled. The Brooke girl is sharper than Ralph. She was very sharp this afternoon. She began at once."

"I—I didn't see her"—wondering.

"Yes, you did; but you didn't understand. The tennis, and the laughing with young Heriot on the terrace! She is going to be the piquant young woman who aggravates by indifference, and disdains rank and splendour; the kind of girl who has her innings in novelettes—but not out of them. The successful women are those who know how to toady in the right way and not obviously. Walderhurst has far too good an opinion of himself to be attracted by a girl who is making up to another man: he's not five-and-twenty."

Emily Fox-Seton was reminded, in spite of herself, of Mrs. Brooke's plaint: "Don't be too indifferent, Cora." She did not want to recall it exactly, because she thought the Brookes agreeable and would have preferred to think them disinterested. But, after all, she reflected, how natural that a girl who was so pretty should feel that the Marquis of Walderhurst represented prospects. Chiefly, however, she was filled with admiration at Lady Maria's cleverness.

"How wonderfully you observe everything, Lady Maria!" she exclaimed. "How wonderfully!"

"I have had forty-seven seasons in London. That's a good many, you know. Forty-seven seasons of débutantes and mothers tend toward enlightenment. Now there is Agatha Slade, poor girl! She's of a kind I know by heart. With birth and beauty, she is perfectly helpless. Her people are poor enough to be entitled to aid from the Charity Organisation, and they have had the indecency to present themselves with six daughters—six! All with delicate skins and delicate little noses and heavenly eyes. Most men can't afford them, and they can't afford most men. As soon as Agatha begins to go off a little, she will have to step aside, if she has not married. The others must be allowed their chance. Agatha has had the advertising of the illustrated papers this season, and she has gone well. In these days a new beauty is advertised like a new soap. They haven't given them sandwich-men in the streets, but that is about all that has been denied them. But Agatha has not had any special offer, and I know both she and her mother are a little frightened. Alix must come out next season, and they can't afford frocks for two. Agatha will have to be sent to their place in Ireland, and to be sent to Castle Clare is almost like being sent to the Bastille. She'll never get out alive. She'll have to stay there and see herself grow thin instead of slim, and colourless instead of fair. Her little nose will grow sharp, and she will lose her hair by degrees."

"Oh!" Emily Fox-Seton gave forth sympathetically. "What a pity that would be! I thought—I really thought—Lord Walderhurst seemed to admire her."

"Oh, every one admires her, for that matter; but if they go no further that will not save her from the Bastille, poor thing. There, Emily; we must go to bed. We have talked enough."

Chapter
Three

To awaken in a still, delicious room, with the summer morning sunshine breaking softly into it through leafy greenness, was a delightful thing to Miss Fox-Seton, who was accustomed to opening her eyes upon four walls covered with cheap paper, to the sound of outside hammerings, and the rattle and heavy roll of wheels. In a building at the back of her bed-sitting-room there lived a man whose occupation, beginning early in the morning, involved banging of a persistent nature.

She awakened to her first day at Mallowe, stretching herself luxuriously, with the smile of a child. She was so thankful for the softness of her lavender-fragrant bed, and so delighted with the lovely freshness of her chintz-hung room. As she lay upon her pillow, she could see the boughs of the trees, and hear the chatter of darting starlings. When her morning tea was brought, it seemed like nectar to her. She was a perfectly healthy woman, with a palate as unspoiled as that of a six-year-old child in the nursery. Her enjoyment of all things was so normal as to be in her day and time an absolute abnormality.

She rose and dressed at once, eager for the open air and sunshine. She was out upon the lawn before anyone else but the Borzoi, which rose from beneath a tree and came with stately walk toward her. The air was exquisite, the broad, beautiful stretch of view lay warm in the sun, the masses of flowers on the herbaceous borders showed leaves and flower-cups adorned with glittering drops of dew. She walked across the spacious sweep of short-cropped sod, and gazed enraptured at the country spread out below. She could have kissed the soft white sheep dotting the fields and lying in gentle, huddled groups under the trees.

"The darlings!" she said, in a little, effusive outburst.

She talked to the dog and fondled him. He seemed to understand her mood, and pressed close against her gown when she stopped. They walked together about the gardens, and presently picked up an exuberant retriever, which bounded and wriggled and at once settled into a steady trot beside them. Emily adored the flowers as she walked by their beds, and at intervals stopped to bury her face in bunches of spicy things. She was so happy that the joy in her hazel eyes was pathetic.

She was startled, as she turned into a rather narrow rose-walk, to see Lord Walderhurst coming toward her. He looked exceedingly clean in his fresh light knickerbocker suit, which was rather becoming to him. A gardener was walking behind, evidently gathering roses for him, which he put into a shallow basket. Emily Fox-Seton cast about for a suitable remark to make, if he should chance to stop to speak to her. She consoled herself with the thought that there were things she really *wanted* to say about the beauty of the gardens, and certain clumps of heavenly-blue campanulas, which seemed made a feature of in the herbaceous borders. It was so much nicer not to be obliged to invent observations. But his lordship did not stop to speak to her. He was interested in his roses (which, she heard afterward, were to be sent to town to an invalid friend), and as she drew near, he turned aside to speak to the gardener. As Emily was just passing him when he turned again, and as the passage was narrow, he found himself unexpectedly gazing into her face.

Being nearly the same height, they were so near each other that it was a little awkward.

"I beg pardon," he said, stepping back a pace and lifting his straw hat.

But he did not say, "I beg pardon, Miss Fox-Seton," and Emily knew that he had not recognised her again, and had not the remotest idea who she was or where she came from.

She passed him with her agreeable, friendly smile, and there returned to her mind Lady Maria's remarks of the night before.

"To think that if he married poor pretty Lady Agatha she will be mistress of three places quite as beautiful as Mallowe, three lovely old houses, three sets of gardens, with thousands of flowers to bloom every year! How nice it would be for her! She is so lovely that it seems as if he *must* fall in love with her.

Then, if she was Marchioness of Walderhurst, she could do so much for her sisters."

After breakfast she spent her morning in doing a hundred things for Lady Maria. She wrote notes for her, and helped her to arrange plans for the entertainment of her visitors. She was very busy and happy. In the afternoon she drove across the moor to Maundell, a village on the other side of it. She really went on an errand for her hostess, but as she was fond of driving and the brown cob was a beauty, she felt that she was being given a treat on a level with the rest of her ladyship's generous hospitalities. She drove well, and her straight, strong figure showed to much advantage on the high seat of the cart. Lord Walderhurst himself commented on her as he saw her drive away.

"She has a nice, flat, straight back, that woman," he remarked to Lady Maria. "What is her name? One never hears people's names when one is introduced."

"Her name is Emily Fox-Seton," her ladyship answered, "and she's a nice creature."

"That would be an inhuman thing to say to most men, but if one is a thoroughly selfish being, and has some knowledge of one's own character, one sees that a nice creature might be a nice companion."

"You are quite right," was Lady Maria's reply, as she held up her lorgnette and watched the cart spin down the avenue. "I am selfish myself, and I realise that is the reason why Emily Fox-Seton is becoming the lodestar of my existence. There is such comfort in being pandered to by a person who is not even aware that she is pandering. She doesn't suspect that she is entitled to thanks for it."

That evening Mrs. Ralph came shining to dinner in amber satin, which seemed to possess some quality of stimulating her to brilliance. She was witty enough to collect an audience, and Lord Walderhurst was drawn within it. This was Mrs. Ralph's evening. When the men returned to the drawing-room, she secured his lordship at once and managed to keep him. She was a woman who could talk pretty well, and perhaps Lord Walderhurst was amused. Emily Fox-Seton was not quite sure that he was, but at least he listened. Lady Agatha Slade looked a little listless and pale. Lovely as she was, she did not always collect an audience, and this evening she said she had a headache. She actually crossed the room, and taking a seat by Miss Emily Fox-Seton, began to talk to her about Lady Maria's charity-knitting which she had taken up. Emily was so gratified that she found conversation easy. She did not realise that at that particular moment she was a most agreeable and comforting companion for Agatha Slade. She had heard so much of her beauty during the season, and remembered so many little things that a girl who was a thought depressed might like to hear referred to again. Sometimes to Agatha the balls where people had collected in groups to watch her dancing, the flattering speeches she had heard, the dazzling hopes which had been raised, seemed a little unreal, as if, after all, they could have been only dreams. This was particularly so, of course, when life had dulled for a while and the atmosphere of unpaid bills became heavy at home. It was so to-day, because the girl had received a long, anxious letter from her mother, in which much was said of the importance of an early preparation for the presentation of Alix, who had really been kept back a year, and was in fact nearer twenty than nineteen.

"If we were not in Debrett and Burke, one might be reserved about such matters," poor Lady Claraway wrote; "but what is one to do when all the world can buy one's daughters' ages at the book-sellers'?"

Miss Fox-Seton had seen Lady Agatha's portrait at the Academy and the way in which people had crowded about it. She had chanced to hear comments also, and she agreed with a number of persons who had not thought the picture did the original justice.

"Sir Bruce Norman was standing by me with an elderly lady the first time I saw it," she said, as she turned a new row of the big white-wool scarf her hostess was knitting for a Deep-Sea Fisherman's Charity. "He really looked quite annoyed. I heard him say: 'It is not good at all. She is far, far lovelier. Her eyes are like blue flowers.' The moment I saw you, I found myself looking at your eyes. I hope I didn't seem rude."

Lady Agatha smiled. She had flushed delicately, and took up in her slim hand a skein of the white wool.

"There are some people who are never rude," she sweetly said, "and you are one of them, I am sure. That knitting looks nice. I wonder if I could make a comforter for a deep-sea fisherman."

"If it would amuse you to try," Emily answered, "I will begin one for you. Lady Maria has several pairs of wooden needles. Shall I?"

"Do, please. How kind of you!"

In a pause of her conversation, Mrs. Ralph, a little later, looked across the room at Emily Fox-Seton bending over Lady Agatha and the knitting, as she gave her instructions.

"What a good-natured creature that is!" she said.

Lord Walderhurst lifted his monocle and inserted it in his unillumined eye. He also looked across the room. Emily wore the black evening dress which gave such opportunities to her square white shoulders and firm column of throat; the country air and sun had deepened the colour on her cheek, and the light of the nearest lamp fell kindly on the big twist of her nut-brown hair, and burnished it. She looked soft and warm, and so generously interested in her pupil's progress that she was rather sweet.

Lord Walderhurst simply looked at her. He was a man of but few words. Women who were sprightly found him somewhat unresponsive. In fact, he was aware that a man in his position need not exert himself. The women themselves would talk. They wanted to talk because they wanted him to hear them.

Mrs. Ralph talked.

"She is the most primeval person I know. She accepts her fate without a trace of resentment; she simply accepts it."

"What is her fate?" asked Lord Walderhurst, still gazing in his unbiassed manner through his monocle, and not turning his head as he spoke.

"It is her fate to be a woman who is perfectly well born, and who is as penniless as a charwoman, and works like one. She is at the beck and call of anyone who will give her an odd job to earn a meal with. That is one of the new ways women have found of making a living."

"Good skin," remarked Lord Walderhurst, irrelevantly. "Good hair—quite a lot."

"She has some of the nicest blood in England in her veins, and she engaged my last cook for me," said Mrs. Ralph.

"Hope she was a good cook."

"Very. Emily Fox-Seton has a faculty of finding decent people. I believe it is because she is so decent herself"—with a little laugh.

"Looks quite decent," commented Walderhurst. The knitting was getting on famously.

"It was odd you should see Sir Bruce Norman that day," Agatha Slade was saying. "It must have been just before he was called away to India."

"It was. He sailed the next day. I happen to know, because some friends of mine met me only a few yards from your picture and began to talk about him. I had not known before that he was so rich. I had not heard about his collieries in Lancashire. Oh!"—opening her big eyes in heart-felt yearning,—"how I wish I owned a colliery! It must be so *nice* to be rich!"

"I never was rich," answered Lady Agatha, with a bitter little sigh. "I know it is hideous to be poor."

"*I* never was rich," said Emily, "and I never shall be. You"—a little shyly—"are so different."

Lady Agatha flushed delicately again.

Emily Fox-Seton made a gentle joke. "You have eyes like blue flowers," she said. Lady Agatha lifted the eyes like blue flowers, and they were pathetic.

"Oh!" she gave forth almost impetuously, "sometimes it seems as if it does not matter whether one has eyes or not."

It was a pleasure to Emily Fox-Seton to realise that after this the beauty seemed to be rather drawn toward her. Their acquaintance became almost a sort of intimacy over the wool scarf for the deep-sea fisherman, which was taken up and laid down, and even carried out on the lawn and left under the trees for the footmen to restore when they brought in the rugs and cushions. Lady Maria was amusing herself with the making of knitted scarves and helmets just now, and bits of white or gray knitting were the fashion at Mallowe. Once Agatha brought hers to Emily's room in the afternoon to ask that a dropped stitch might be taken up, and this established a sort of precedent. Afterward they began to exchange visits.

The strenuousness of things was becoming, in fact, almost too much for Lady Agatha. Most unpleasant things were happening at home, and occasionally Castle Clare loomed up grayly in the distance like a spectre. Certain tradespeople who ought, in Lady Claraway's opinion, to have kept quiet and waited in patience until things became better, were becoming hideously persistent. In view of the fact that Alix's next season must be provided for, it was most awkward. A girl could not be presented and properly launched in the world, in a way which would give her a proper chance, without expenditure. To the Claraways expenditure meant credit, and there were blots as of tears on the letters in which Lady Claraway reiterated that the tradespeople were behaving horribly. Sometimes, she said once in desperation, things looked as if they would all be obliged to shut themselves up in Castle Clare to retrench; and then what was to become of Alix and her season? And there were Millicent and Hilda and Eve.

More than once there was the mist of tears in the flower-blue eyes when Lady Agatha came to talk. Confidence between two women establishes itself through processes at once subtle and simple. Emily Fox-Seton could not have told when she first began to know that the beauty was troubled and distressed; Lady Agatha did not know when she first slipped into making little frank speeches about herself; but these things came about. Agatha found something like comfort in her acquaintance with the big, normal, artless creature—something which actually raised her spirits when she was depressed. Emily Fox-Seton paid constant kindly tribute to her charms, and helped her to believe in them. When she was with her, Agatha always felt that she really was lovely, after all, and that loveliness was a great capital. Emily admired and revered it so, and evidently never dreamed of doubting its omnipotence. She used to talk as if any girl who was a beauty was a potential duchess. In fact, this was a thing she quite ingenuously believed. She had not lived in a world where marriage was a thing of romance, and, for that matter, neither had Agatha. It was nice if a girl liked the man who married her, but if he was a well-behaved, agreeable person, of good means, it was natural that she would end by liking him sufficiently; and to be provided for comfortably or luxuriously for life, and not left upon one's own hands or one's parents', was a thing to be thankful for in any case. It was such a relief to everybody to know that a girl was "settled," and especially it was such a relief to the girl herself. Even novels and plays were no longer fairy-stories of entrancing young men and captivating young women who fell in love with each other in the first chapter, and after increasingly picturesque incidents were married in the last one in the absolute surety of being blissfully happy forevermore. Neither Lady Agatha nor Emily had been brought up on this order of literature, nor in an atmosphere in which it was accepted without reservation.

They had both had hard lives, and knew what lay before them. Agatha knew she must make a marriage or fade out of existence in prosaic and narrowed dulness. Emily knew that there was no prospect for her of desirable marriage at all. She was too poor, too entirely unsupported by social surroundings, and not sufficiently radiant to catch the roving eye. To be able to maintain herself decently, to be given an occasional treat by her more fortunate friends, and to be allowed by fortune to present to the face of the world the appearance of a woman who was not a pauper, was all she could expect. But she felt that Lady Agatha had the right to more. She did not reason the matter out and ask herself why she had the right to more, but she accepted the proposition as a fact. She was ingenuously interested in her fate, and affectionately sympathetic. She used to look at Lord Walderhurst quite anxiously at times when he was talking to the girl. An anxious mother could scarcely have regarded him with a greater desire to analyse his sentiments. The match would be such a fitting one. He would make such an excellent husband—and there were three places, and the diamonds were magnificent. Lady Maria had described to her a certain tiara which she frequently pictured to herself as glittering above Agatha's exquisite low brow. It would be infinitely more becoming to her than to Miss Brooke or Mrs. Ralph, though either of them would have worn it with spirit. She could not help feeling that both Mrs. Ralph's brilliancy and Miss Brooke's insouciant prettiness were not unworthy of being counted in the running, but Lady Agatha seemed somehow so much more completely the thing wanted. She was anxious that she should always look her best, and when she knew that disturbing letters were fretting her, and saw that they made her look pale and less luminous, she tried to raise her spirits.

"Suppose we take a brisk walk," she would say, "and then you might try a little nap. You look a little tired."

"Oh," said Agatha one day, "how kind you are to me! I believe you actually care about my complexion—about my looking well."

"Lord Walderhurst said to me the other day," was Emily's angelically tactful answer, "that you were the only woman he had ever seen who *always* looked lovely."

"Did he?" exclaimed Lady Agatha, and flushed sweetly. "Once Sir Bruce Norman actually said that to me. I told him it was the nicest thing that could be said to a woman. It is all the nicer"—with a sigh—"because it isn't *really* true."

"I am sure Lord Walderhurst believed it true," Emily said. "He is not a man who talks, you know. He is very serious and dignified." She had herself a reverence and admiration for Lord Walderhurst bordering on tender awe. He was indeed a well-mannered person, of whom painful things were not said. He also conducted himself well toward his tenantry, and was patron of several notable charities. To the unexacting and innocently respectful mind of Emily Fox-Seton this was at once impressive and attractive. She knew, though not intimately, many noble personages quite unlike him. She was rather early Victorian and touchingly respectable.

"I have been crying," confessed Lady Agatha.

"I was afraid so, Lady Agatha," said Emily.

"Things are getting hopeless in Curzon Street. I had a letter from Millicent this morning. She is next in age to Alix, and she says—oh, a number of things. When girls see everything passing by them, it makes them irritable. Millicent is seventeen, and she is too lovely. Her hair is like a red-gold cloak, and her eyelashes are twice as long as mine." She sighed again, and her lips, which were like curved rose-petals, unconcealedly quivered. "They were *all* so cross about Sir Bruce Norman going to India," she added.

"He will come back," said Emily, benignly; "but he may be too late. Has he"—ingenuously—"seen Alix?"

Agatha flushed oddly this time. Her delicate skin registered every emotion exquisitely. "He has seen her, but she was in the school-room, and—I don't think—"

She did not finish, but stopped uneasily, and sat and gazed out of the open window into the park. She did not look happy.

The episode of Sir Bruce Norman was brief and even vague. It had begun well. Sir Bruce had met the beauty at a ball, and they had danced together more than once. Sir Bruce had attractions other than his old baronetcy and his coal-mines. He was a good-looking person, with a laughing brown eye and a nice wit. He had danced charmingly and paid gay compliments. He would have done immensely well. Agatha had liked him. Emily sometimes thought she had liked him very much. Her mother had liked him and had thought he was attracted. But after a number of occasions of agreeable meetings, they had encountered each other on the lawn at Goodwood, and he had announced that he was going to India. Forthwith he had gone, and Emily had gathered that somehow Lady Agatha had been considered somewhat to blame. Her people were not vulgar enough to express this frankly, but she had felt it. Her younger sisters had, upon the whole, made her feel it most. It had been borne in upon her that if Alix, or Millicent with the red-gold cloak, or even Eve, who was a gipsy, had been given such a season and such Doucet frocks, they would have combined them with their wonderful complexions and lovely little chins and noses in such a manner as would at least have prevented desirable acquaintances from feeling free to take P. and O. steamers to Bombay.

In her letter of this morning, Millicent's temper had indeed got somewhat the better of her taste and breeding, and lovely Agatha had cried large tears. So it was comforting to be told that Lord Walderhurst had said such an extremely amiable thing. If he was not young, he was really *very* nice, and there were exalted persons who absolutely had rather a fad for him. It would be exceptionally brilliant.

The brisk walk was taken, and Lady Agatha returned from it blooming. She was adorable at dinner, and in the evening gathered an actual court about her. She was all in pink, and a wreath of little pink wild roses lay close about her head, making her, with her tall young slimness, look like a Botticelli nymph. Emily saw that Lord Walderhurst looked at her a great deal. He sat on an extraordinarily comfortable corner seat, and stared through his monocle.

Lady Maria always gave her Emily plenty to do. She had a nice taste in floral arrangement, and early in her visit it had fallen into her hands as a duty to "do" the flowers.

The next morning she was in the gardens early, gathering roses with the dew on them, and was in the act of cutting some adorable "Mrs. Sharman Crawfords," when she found it behooved her to let down her carefully tucked up petticoats, as the Marquis of Walderhurst was walking straight toward her. An instinct told her that he wanted to talk to her about Lady Agatha Slade.

"You get up earlier than Lady Agatha," he remarked, after he had wished her "Good-morning."

"She is oftener invited to the country than I am," she answered. "When I have a country holiday, I want to spend every moment of it out of doors. And the mornings are so lovely. They are not like this in Mortimer Street."

"Do you live in Mortimer Street?"

"Yes."

"Do you like it?"

"I am very comfortable. I am fortunate in having a nice landlady. She and her daughter are very kind to me."

The morning was indeed heavenly. The masses of flowers were drenched with dew, and the already hot sun was drawing fragrance from them and filling the warm air with it. The marquis, with his monocle fixed, looked up into the cobalt-blue sky and among the trees, where a wood-dove or two cooed with musical softness.

"Yes," he observed, with a glance which swept the scene, "it is different from Mortimer Street, I suppose. Are you fond of the country?"

"Oh, yes," sighed Emily; "oh, yes!"

She was not a specially articulate person. She could not have conveyed in words all that her "Oh, yes!" really meant of simple love for and joy in rural sights and sounds and scents. But when she lifted her big kind hazel eyes to him, the earnestness of her emotion made them pathetic, as the unspeakableness of her pleasures often did.

Lord Walderhurst gazed at her through the monocle with an air he sometimes had of taking her measure without either unkindliness or particular interest.

"Is Lady Agatha fond of the country?" he inquired.

"She is fond of everything that is beautiful," she replied. "Her nature is as lovely as her face, I think."

"Is it?"

Emily walked a step or two away to a rose climbing up the gray-red wall, and began to clip off blossoms, which tumbled sweetly into her basket.

"She seems lovely in everything," she said, "in disposition and manner and—everything. She never seems to disappoint one or make mistakes."

"You are fond of her?"

"She has been so kind to me."

"You often say people are kind to you."

Emily paused and felt a trifle confused. Realising that she was not a clever person, and being a modest one, she began to wonder if she was given to a parrot-phrase which made her tiresome. She blushed up to her ears.

"People are kind," she said hesitatingly. "I—you see, I have nothing to give, and I always seem to be receiving."

"What luck!" remarked his lordship, calmly gazing at her.

He made her feel rather awkward, and she was at once relieved and sorry when he walked away to join another early riser who had come out upon the lawn. For some mysterious reason Emily Fox-Seton liked him. Perhaps his magnificence and the constant talk she had heard of him had warmed her imagination. He had never said anything particularly intelligent to her, but she felt as if he had. He was a rather silent man, but never looked stupid. He had made some good speeches in the House of Lords, not brilliant, but sound and of a dignified respectability. He had also written two pamphlets. Emily had an enormous respect for intellect, and frequently, it must be admitted, for the thing which passed for it. She was not exacting.

During her stay at Mallowe in the summer, Lady Maria always gave a village treat. She had given it for forty years, and it was a lively function. Several hundred wildly joyous village children were fed to repletion with exhilarating buns and cake, and tea in mugs, after which they ran races for prizes, and were entertained in various ways, with the aid of such of the house-party as were benevolently inclined to make themselves useful.

Everybody was not so inclined, though people always thought the thing amusing. Nobody objected to looking on, and some were agreeably stimulated by the general sense of festivity. But Emily Fox-Seton was found by Lady Maria to be invaluable on this occasion. It was so easy, without the least sense of ill-feeling, to give her all the drudgery to do. There was plenty of drudgery, though it did not present itself to Emily Fox-Seton in that light. She no more realised that she was giving Lady Maria a good deal for her money, so to speak, than she realised that her ladyship, though an amusing and delightful, was an absolutely selfish and inconsiderate old woman. So long as Emily Fox-Seton did not seem obviously tired, it would not have occurred to Lady Maria that she could be so; that, after all, her legs and arms were mere human flesh and blood, that her substantial feet were subject to the fatigue unending trudging to and fro induces. Her ladyship was simply delighted that the preparations went so well, that she could turn to Emily for service and always find her ready. Emily made lists and calculations; she worked out plans and made purchases. She interviewed the village matrons who made the cake and buns, and boiled the tea in bags in a copper; she found the women who could be engaged to assist in cutting cake and bread-and-butter and helping to serve it; she ordered the putting up of tents and forms and tables; the innumerable things to be remembered she called to mind.

"Really, Emily," said Lady Maria, "I don't know how I have done this thing for forty years without you. I must always have you at Mallowe for the treat."

Emily was of the genial nature which rejoices upon even small occasions, and is invariably stimulated to pleasure by the festivities of others. The festal atmosphere was a delight to her. In her numberless errands to the village, the sight of the excitement in the faces of the children she passed on her way to this cottage and that filled her eyes with friendly glee and wreathed her face with smiles. When she went into the cottage where the cake was being baked, children hovered about in groups and nudged each other, giggling. They hung about, partly through thrilled interest, and partly because their joy made them eager to courtesy to her as she came out, the obeisance seeming to identify them even more closely with the coming treat. They grinned and beamed rosily, and Emily smiled at them and nodded, uplifted by a pleasure almost as infantile as their own. She was really enjoying herself so honestly that she did not realise how hard she worked during the days before the festivity. She was really ingenious, and invented a number of new methods of entertainment. It was she who, with the aid of a couple of gardeners, transformed the tents into bowers of green boughs and arranged the decorations of the tables and the park gates.

"What a lot of walking you do!" Lord Walderhurst said to her once, as she passed the group on the lawn. "Do you know how many hours you have been on your feet to-day?"

"I like it," she answered, and, as she hurried by, she saw that he was sitting a shade nearer to Lady Agatha than she had ever seen him sit before, and that Agatha, under a large hat of white gauze frills, was looking like a seraph, so sweet and shining were her eyes, so flower-fair her face. She looked actually happy.

"Perhaps he has been saying things," Emily thought. "How happy she will be! He has such a nice pair of eyes. He would make a woman very happy." A faint sigh fluttered from her lips. She was beginning to be physically tired, and was not yet quite aware of it. If she had not been physically tired, she would not even vaguely have had, at this moment, recalled to her mind the fact that she was not of the women to whom "things" are said and to whom things happen.

"Emily Fox-Seton," remarked Lady Maria, fanning herself, as it was frightfully hot, "has the most admirable effect on me. She makes me feel generous. I should like to present her with the smartest things from the wardrobes of all my relations."

"Do you give her clothes?" asked Walderhurst.

"I haven't any to spare. But I know they would be useful to her. The things she wears are touching; they are so well contrived, and produce such a decent effect with so little."

Lord Walderhurst inserted his monocle and gazed after the straight, well-set-up back of the disappearing Miss Fox-Seton.

"I think," said Lady Agatha, gently, "that she is really handsome."

"So she is," admitted Walderhurst—"quite a good-looking woman."

That night Lady Agatha repeated the amiability to Emily, whose grateful amazement really made her blush.

"Lord Walderhurst knows Sir Bruce Norman," said Agatha. "Isn't it strange? He spoke of him to me to-day. He says he is clever."

"You had a nice talk this afternoon, hadn't you?" said Emily. "You both looked so—so—as if you were enjoying yourselves when I passed."

"Did he look as if he were enjoying himself? He was very agreeable. I did not know he could be so agreeable."

"I have never seen him look as much pleased," answered Emily Fox-Seton. "Though he always looks as if he liked talking to you, Lady Agatha. That large white gauze garden-hat"—reflectively—"is so *very* becoming."

"It was very expensive," sighed lovely Agatha. "And they last such a short time. Mamma said it really seemed almost criminal to buy it."

"How delightful it will be," remarked cheering Emily, "when—when you need not think of things like that!"

"Oh!"—with another sigh, this time a catch of the breath,—"it would be like Heaven! People don't know; they think girls are frivolous when they care, and that it isn't serious. But when one knows one *must* have things,—that they are like bread,—it is awful!"

"The things you wear really matter." Emily was bringing all her powers to bear upon the subject, and with an anxious kindness which was quite angelic. "Each dress makes you look like another sort of picture. Have you,"—contemplatively—"anything *quite* different to wear to-night and to-morrow?"

"I have two evening dresses I have not worn here yet"—a little hesitatingly. "I—well I saved them. One is a very thin black one with silver on it. It has a trembling silver butterfly for the shoulder, and one for the hair."

"Oh, put that on to-night!" said Emily, eagerly. "When you come down to dinner you will look so—so new! I always think that to see a fair person suddenly for the first time all in black gives one a kind of delighted start—though start isn't the word, quite. Do put it on."

Lady Agatha put it on. Emily Fox-Seton came into her room to help to add the last touches to her beauty before she went down to dinner. She suggested that the fair hair should be dressed even higher and more lightly than usual, so that the silver butterfly should poise the more airily over the knot, with its quivering, outstretched wings. She herself poised the butterfly high upon the shoulder.

"Oh, it is lovely!" she exclaimed, drawing back to gaze at the girl. "Do let me go down a moment or so before you do, so that I can see you come into the room."

She was sitting in a chair quite near Lord Walderhurst when her charge entered. She saw him really give something quite like a start when Agatha appeared. His monocle, which had been in his eye, fell out of it, and he picked it up by its thin cord and replaced it.

"Psyche!" she heard him say in his odd voice, which seemed merely to make a statement without committing him to an opinion—"Psyche!"

He did not say it to her or to anyone else. It was simply a kind of exclamation,—appreciative and perceptive without being enthusiastic,—and it was curious. He talked to Agatha nearly all the evening.

Emily came to Lady Agatha before she retired, looking even a little flushed.

"What are you going to wear at the treat to-morrow?" she asked.

"A white muslin, with *entre-deux* of lace, and the gauze garden-hat, and a white parasol and shoes."

Lady Agatha looked a little nervous; her pink fluttered in her cheek.

"And to-morrow night?" said Emily.

"I have a very pale blue. Won't you sit down, dear Miss Fox-Seton?"

"We must both go to bed and sleep. You must not get tired."

But she sat down for a few minutes, because she saw the girl's eyes asking her to do it.

The afternoon post had brought a more than usually depressing letter from Curzon Street. Lady Claraway was at her motherly wits' ends, and was really quite touching in her distraction. A dressmaker was entering a suit. The thing would get into the papers, of course.

"Unless something happens, something to save us by staving off things, we shall have to go to Castle

Clare at once. It will be all over. No girl could be presented with such a thing in the air. They don't like it."

"They," of course, meant persons whose opinions made London's society's law.

"To go to Castle Clare," faltered Agatha, "will be like being sentenced to starve to death. Alix and Hilda and Millicent and Eve and I will be starved, quite slowly, for the want of the things that make girls' lives bearable when they have been born in a certain class. And even if the most splendid thing happened in three or four years, it would be too late for us four—almost too late for Eve. If you are out of London, of course you are forgotten. People can't help forgetting. Why shouldn't they, when there are such crowds of new girls every year?"

Emily Fox-Seton was sweet. She was quite sure that they would not be obliged to go to Castle Clare. Without being indelicate, she was really able to bring hope to the fore. She said a good deal of the black gauze dress and the lovely effect of the silver butterflies.

"I suppose it was the butterflies which made Lord Walderhurst say 'Psyche! Psyche!' when he first saw you," she added, *en passant*.

"Did he say that?" And immediately Lady Agatha looked as if she had not intended to say the words.

"Yes," answered Emily, hurrying on with a casual air which had a good deal of tact in it. "And black makes you so wonderfully fair and aërial. You scarcely look quite real in it; you might float away. But you must go to sleep now."

Lady Agatha went with her to the door of the room to bid her good-night. Her eyes looked like those of a child who might presently cry a little. "Oh, Miss Fox-Seton," she said, in a very young voice, "you are so kind!"

Chapter
Four

The parts of the park nearest to the house already presented a busy aspect when Miss Fox-Seton passed through the gardens the following morning. Tables were being put up, and baskets of bread and cake and groceries were being carried into the tent where the tea was to be prepared. The workers looked interested and good-humoured; the men touched their hats as Emily appeared, and the women curtsied smilingly. They had all discovered that she was amiable and to be relied on in her capacity of her ladyship's representative.

"She's a worker, that Miss Fox-Seton," one said to the other. "I never seen one that was a lady fall to as she does. Ladies, even when they means well, has a way of standing about and telling you to do things without seeming to know quite how they ought to be done. She's coming to help with the bread-and-butter-cutting herself this morning, and she put up all them packages of sweets yesterday with her own hands. She did 'em up in different-coloured papers, and tied 'em with bits of ribbon, because she said she knowed children was prouder of coloured things than plain—they was like that. And so they are: a bit of red or blue goes a long way with a child."

Emily cut bread-and-butter and cake, and placed seats and arranged toys on tables all the morning. The day was hot, though beautiful, and she was so busy that she had scarcely time for her breakfast. The household party was in the gayest spirits. Lady Maria was in her most amusing mood. She had planned a drive to some interesting ruins for the afternoon of the next day, and a dinner-party for the evening. Her favourite neighbours had just returned to their country-seat five miles away, and they were coming to the dinner, to her great satisfaction. Most of her neighbours bored her, and she took them in doses at her dinners, as she would have taken medicine. But the Lockyers were young and good-looking and clever, and she was always glad when they came to Loche during her stay at Mallowe.

"There is not a frump or a bore among them," she said. "In the country people are usually frumps when they are not bores, and bores when they are not frumps, and I am in danger of becoming both myself. Six weeks of unalloyed dinner-parties, composed of certain people I know, would make me begin to wear moreen petticoats and talk about the deplorable condition of London society."

She led all her flock out on to the lawn under the ilex-trees after breakfast.

"Let us go and encourage industry," she said. "We will watch Emily Fox-Seton working. She is an example."

Curiously enough, this was Miss Cora Brooke's day. She found herself actually walking across the lawn with Lord Walderhurst by her side. She did not know how it happened, but it seemed to occur accidentally.

"We never talk to each other," he said.

"Well," answered Cora, "we have talked to other people a great deal—at least I have."

"Yes, you have talked a good deal," said the marquis.

"Does that mean I have talked too much?"

He surveyed her prettiness through his glass. Perhaps the holiday stir in the air gave him a festive moment.

"It means that you haven't talked enough to me. You have devoted yourself too much to the laying low of young Heriot."

She laughed a trifle saucily.

"You are a very independent young lady," remarked Walderhurst, with a lighter manner than usual. "You ought to say something deprecatory or— a little coy, perhaps."

"I shan't," said Cora, composedly.

"Shan't or won't?" he inquired. "They are both bad words for little girls—or young ladies—to use to their elders."

"Both," said Miss Cora Brooke, with a slightly pleased flush. "Let us go over to the tents and see what poor Emily Fox-Seton is doing."

"Poor Emily Fox-Seton," said the marquis, non-committally.

They went, but they did not stay long. The treat was taking form. Emily Fox-Seton was hot and deeply engaged. People were coming to her for orders. She had a thousand things to do and to superintend the doing of. The prizes for the races and the presents for the children must be arranged in order: things for boys and things for girls, presents for little children and presents for big ones. Nobody must be missed, and no one must be given the wrong thing.

"It would be dreadful, you know," Emily said to the two when they came into her tent and began to ask questions, "if a big boy should get a small wooden horse, or a little baby should be given a cricket bat and ball. Then it would be so disappointing if a tiny girl got a work-box and a big one got a doll. One has to get things in order. They look forward to this so, and it's heart-breaking to a child to be disappointed, isn't it?"

Walderhurst gazed uninspiringly.

"Who did this for Lady Maria when you were not here?" he inquired.

"Oh, other people. But she says it was tiresome." Then with an illumined smile; "She has asked me to Mallowe for the next twenty years for the treats. She is so kind."

"Maria is a kind woman"—with what seemed to Emily delightful amiability. "She is kind to her treats and she is kind to Maria Bayne."

"She is kind to *me*," said Emily. "You don't know how I am enjoying this."

"That woman enjoys everything," Lord Walderhurst said when he walked away with Cora. "What a temperament to have! I would give ten thousand a year for it."

"She has so little," said Cora, "that everything seems beautiful to her. One doesn't wonder, either. She's very nice. Mother and I quite admire her. We are thinking of inviting her to New York and giving her a real good time."

"She would enjoy New York."

"Have you ever been there, Lord Walderhurst?"

"No."

"You ought to come, really. So many Englishmen come now, and they all seem to like it."

"Perhaps I will come," said Walderhurst. "I have been thinking of it. One is tired of the Continent and one knows India. One doesn't know Fifth Avenue, and Central Park, and the Rocky Mountains."

"One might try them," suggested pretty Miss Cora.

This certainly was her day. Lord Walderhurst took her and her mother out in his own particular high phaeton before lunch. He was fond of driving, and his own phaeton and horses had come to Mallowe with him. He took only his favourites out, and though he bore himself on this occasion with a calm air, the event caused a little smiling flurry on the lawn. At least, when the phaeton spun down the avenue with Miss Brooke and her mother looking slightly flushed and thrilled in their high seats of honour, several people exchanged glances and raised eye-brows.

Lady Agatha went to her room and wrote a long letter to Curzon Street. Mrs. Ralph talked about the problem-play to young Heriot and a group of others.

The afternoon, brilliant and blazing, brought new visitors to assist by their presence at the treat. Lady Maria always had a large house-party, and added guests from the neighbourhood to make for gaiety. At two o'clock a procession of village children and their friends and parents, headed by the village band, marched up the avenue and passed before the house on their way to their special part of the park. Lady Maria and her guests stood upon the broad steps and welcomed the jocund crowd, as it moved by, with hospitable bows and nods and becks and wreathed smiles. Everybody was in a delighted good-humour.

As the villagers gathered in the park, the house-party joined them by way of the gardens. A conjurer from London gave an entertainment under a huge tree, and children found white rabbits taken from their pockets and oranges from their caps, with squeals of joy and shouts of laughter. Lady Maria's guests walked about and looked on, laughing with the children.

The great affair of tea followed the performance. No treat is fairly under way until the children are filled to the brim with tea and buns and cake, principally cake in plummy wedges.

Lady Agatha and Mrs. Ralph handed cake along rows of children seated on the grass. Miss Brooke was talking to Lord Walderhurst when the work began. She had poppies in her hat and carried a poppy-coloured parasol, and sat under a tree, looking very alluring.

"I ought to go and help to hand cake," she said.

"My cousin Maria ought to do it," remarked Lord Walderhurst, "but she will not—neither shall I. Tell me something about the elevated railroad and Five-Hundred-and-Fifty-Thousandth Street." He had a slightly rude, gracefully languid air, which Cora Brooke found somewhat impressive, after all.

Emily Fox-Seton handed cake and regulated supplies with cheerful tact and good spirits. When the older people were given their tea, she moved about their tables, attending to everyone. She was too heart-whole in her interest in her hospitalities to find time to join Lady Maria and her party at the table under the ilex-trees. She ate some bread-and-butter and drank a cup of tea while she talked to some old women she had made friends with. She was really enjoying herself immensely, though occasionally she was obliged to sit down for a few moments just to rest her tired feet. The children came to her as to an omnipotent and benign being. She knew where the toys were kept and what prizes were to be given for the races. She represented law and order and bestowal. The other ladies walked about in wonderful dresses, smiling and exalted, the gentlemen aided the sports in an amateurish way and made patrician jokes among themselves, but this one lady seemed to be part of the treat itself. She was not so grandly dressed as the others,—her dress was only blue linen with white bands on it,—and she had only a sailor hat with a buckle and bow, but she was of her ladyship's world of London people, nevertheless, and they liked her more than they had ever liked a lady before. It was a fine treat, and she seemed to have made it so. There had never been quite such a varied and jovial treat at Mallowe before.

The afternoon waxed and waned. The children played games and raced and rejoiced until their young limbs began to fail them. The older people sauntered about or sat in groups to talk and listen to the village band. Lady Maria's visitors, having had enough of rural festivities, went back to the gardens in excellent spirits, to talk and to watch a game of tennis which had taken form on the court.

Emily Fox-Seton's pleasure had not abated, but her colour had done so. Her limbs ached and her still-smiling face was pale, as she stood under the beech-tree regarding the final ceremonies of the festal day, to preside over which Lady Maria and her party returned from their seats under the ilex-trees. The National Anthem was sung loudly, and there were three tremendous cheers given for her ladyship. They were such joyous and hearty cheers that Emily was stirred almost to emotional tears. At all events, her hazel eyes looked nice and moistly bright. She was an easily moved creature.

Lord Walderhurst stood near Lady Maria and looked pleased also. Emily saw him speak to her ladyship and saw Lady Maria smile. Then he stepped forward, with his non-committal air and his monocle glaring calmly in his eye.

"Boys and girls," he said in a clear, far-reaching voice, "I want you to give three of the biggest cheers you are capable of for the lady who has worked to make your treat the success it has been. Her ladyship tells me she has never had such a treat before. Three cheers for Miss Fox-Seton."

Emily gave a gasp and felt a lump rise in her throat. She felt as if she had been without warning suddenly changed into a royal personage, and she scarcely knew what to do.

The whole treat, juvenile and adult, male and female, burst into three cheers which were roars and bellows Hats and caps were waved and tossed into the air, and every creature turned toward her as she blushed and bowed in tremulous gratitude and delight.

"Oh, Lady Maria! oh, Lord Walderhurst!" she said, when she managed to get to them, "how *kind* you are to me!"

A fter she had taken her early tea in the morning, Emily Fox-Seton lay upon her pillows and gazed out upon the tree-branches near her window, in a state of bliss. She was tired, but happy. How well everything had "gone off"! How pleased Lady Maria had been, and how kind of Lord Walderhurst to ask the villagers to give three cheers for herself! She had never dreamed of such a thing. It was the kind of attention not usually offered to her. She smiled her childlike smile and blushed at the memory of it. Her impression of the world was that people were really very amiable, as a rule. They were always good to her, at least, she thought, and it did not occur to her that if she had not paid her way so remarkably well by being useful they might have been less agreeable. Never once had she doubted that Lady Maria was the most admirable and generous of human beings. She was not aware in the least that her ladyship got a good deal out of her. In justice to her ladyship, it may be said that she was not wholly aware of it herself, and that Emily absolutely enjoyed being made use of.

This morning, however, when she got up, she found herself more tired than she ever remembered being before, and it may be easily argued that a woman who runs about London on other people's errands often knows what it is to be aware of aching limbs. She laughed a little when she discovered that her feet were actually rather swollen, and that she must wear a pair of her easiest slippers. "I must sit down as much as I can to-day," she thought. "And yet, with the dinner-party and the excursion this morning, there may be a number of little things Lady Maria would like me to do."

There were, indeed, numbers of things Lady Maria was extremely glad to ask her to do. The drive to the ruins was to be made before lunch, because some of the guests felt that an afternoon jaunt would leave them rather fagged for the dinner-party in the evening. Lady Maria was not going, and, as presently became apparent, the carriages would be rather crowded if Miss Fox-Seton joined the party. On the whole, Emily was not sorry to have an excuse for remaining at home, and so the carriages drove away comfortably filled, and Lady Maria and Miss Fox-Seton watched their departure.

"I have no intention of having my venerable bones rattled over hill and dale the day I give a dinner-party," said her ladyship. "Please ring the bell, Emily. I want to make sure of the fish. Fish is one of the problems of country life. Fishmongers are demons, and when they live five miles from one they can arouse the most powerful human emotions."

Mallowe Court was at a distance from the country town delightful in its effects upon the rusticity of the neighbourhood, but appalling when considered in connection with fish. One could not dine without fish; the town was small and barren of resources, and the one fishmonger of weak mind and unreliable nature.

The footman who obeyed the summons of the bell informed her ladyship that the cook was rather anxious about the fish, as usual. The fishmonger had been a little doubtful as to whether he could supply her needs, and his cart never arrived until half-past twelve.

"Great goodness!" exclaimed her ladyship when the man retired. "What a situation if we found ourselves without fish! Old General Barnes is the most ferocious old gourmand in England, and he loathes people who give him bad dinners. We are all rather afraid of him, the fact is, and I will own that I am vain about my dinners. That is the last charm nature leaves a woman, the power to give decent dinners. I shall be fearfully annoyed if any ridiculous thing happens."

They sat in the morning-room together writing notes and talking, and as half-past twelve drew near, watching for the fishmonger's cart. Once or twice Lady Maria spoke of Lord Walderhurst.

"He is an interesting creature, to my mind," she said. "I have always rather liked him. He has original ideas, though he is not in the least brilliant. I believe he talks more freely to me, on the whole, than to most people, though I can't say he has a particularly good opinion of me. He stuck his glass in his eye and stared at me last night, in that weird way of his, and said to me, 'Maria, in an ingenuous fashion of your own, you are the most abominably selfish woman I ever beheld.' Still, I know he rather likes me. I said to him: 'That isn't quite true, James. I am selfish, but I'm not *abominably* selfish. Abominably selfish people always have nasty tempers, and no one can accuse me of having a nasty temper. I have the disposition of a bowl of bread and milk."

"Emily,"—as wheels rattled up the avenue,—"*is* that the fishmonger's cart?"

"No," answered Emily at the window; "it is the butcher."

"His attitude toward the women here has made my joy," Lady Maria proceeded, smiling over the deep-sea fishermen's knitted helmet she had taken up. "He behaves beautifully to them all, but not one of them has really a leg to stand on as far as he is responsible for it. But I will tell you something, Emily." She paused.

Miss Fox-Seton waited with interested eyes.

"He is thinking of bringing the thing to an end and marrying *some* woman. I feel it in my bones."

"Do you think so?" exclaimed Emily. "Oh, I can't help hoping—" But she paused also.

"You hope it will be Agatha Slade," Lady Maria ended for her. "Well, perhaps it will be. I sometimes think it is Agatha, if it's any one. And yet I'm not sure. One never could be sure with Walderhurst. He has always had a trick of keeping more than his mouth shut. I wonder if he could have any other woman up his sleeve?"

"Why do you think—" began Emily.

Lady Maria laughed.

"For an odd reason. The Walderhursts have a ridiculously splendid ring in the family, which they have a way of giving to the women they become engaged to. It's ridiculous because—well, because a ruby as big as a trouser's button *is* ridiculous. You can't get over that. There is a story connected with this one—centuries and things, and something about the woman the first Walderhurst had it made for. She was a Dame Something or Other who had snubbed the King for being forward, and the snubbing was so good for him that he thought she was a saint and gave the ruby for her betrothal. Well, by the merest accident I found Walderhurst had sent his man to town for it. It came two days ago."

"Oh, how interesting!" said Emily, thrilled. "It *must* mean something."

"It is rather a joke. Wheels again, Emily. Is *that* the fishmonger?"

Emily went to the window once more. "Yes," she answered, "if his name is Buggle."

"His name *is* Buggle," said Lady Maria, "and we are saved."

But five minutes later the cook herself appeared at the morning-room door. She was a stout person, who panted, and respectfully removed beads of perspiration from her brow with a clean handkerchief.

She was as nearly pale as a heated person of her weight may be.

"And what has happened now, cook?" asked Lady Maria.

"That Buggle, your ladyship," said cook, "says your ladyship can't be no sorrier than he is, but when fish goes bad in a night it can't be made fresh in the morning. He brought it that I might see it for myself, and it is in a state as could not be used by any one. I was that upset, your ladyship, that I felt like I must come and explain myself."

"What *can* be done?" exclaimed Lady Maria. "Emily, *do* suggest something."

"We can't even be sure," said the cook, "that Batch has what would suit us. Batch sometimes has it, but he is the fishmonger at Maundell, and that is four miles away, and we are short-'anded, your ladyship, now the 'ouse is so full, and not a servant that could be spared."

"Dear me!" said Lady Maria. "Emily, this is really enough to drive one quite mad. If everything was not out of the stables, I know you would drive over to Maundell. You are such a good walker,"—catching a gleam of hope,—"do you think you could walk?"

Emily tried to look cheerful. Lady Maria's situation was really an awful one for a hostess. It would not have mattered in the least if her strong, healthy body had not been so tired. She was an excellent walker, and ordinarily eight miles would have meant nothing in the way of fatigue. She was kept in good training by her walking in town, Springy moorland swept by fresh breezes was not like London streets.

"I think I can manage it," she said nice-temperedly. "If I had not run about so much yesterday it would be a mere nothing. You must have the fish, of course. I will walk over the moor to Maundell and tell Batch it must be sent at once. Then

I will come back slowly. I can rest on the heather by the way. The moor is lovely in the afternoon."

"You dear soul!" Lady Maria broke forth. "What a boon you are to a woman!"

She felt quite grateful. There arose in her mind an impulse to invite Emily Fox-Seton to remain the rest of her life with her, but she was too experienced an elderly lady to give way to impulses. She privately resolved, however, that she would have her a good deal in South Audley Street, and would make her some decent presents.

When Emily Fox-Seton, attired for her walk in her shortest brown linen frock and shadiest hat, passed through the hall, the post-boy was just delivering the midday letters to a footman. The servant presented his salver to her with a letter for herself lying upon the top of one addressed in Lady Claraway's handwriting "To the Lady Agatha Slade." Emily recognised it as one of the epistles of many sheets which so often made poor Agatha shed slow and depressed tears. Her own letter was directed in the well-known hand of Mrs. Cupp, and she wondered what it could contain.

"I hope the poor things are not in any trouble," she thought. "They were afraid the young man in the sitting-room was engaged. If he got married and left them, I don't know what they would do; he has been so regular."

Though the day was hot, the weather was perfect, and Emily, having exchanged her easy slippers for an almost equally easy pair of tan shoes, found her tired feet might still be used. Her disposition to make the very best of things inspired her to regard even an eight-mile walk with courage. The moorland air was so sweet, the sound of the bees droning as they stumbled about in the heather was such a comfortable, peaceful thing, that she convinced herself that she should find the four miles to Maundell quite agreeable.

She had so many nice things to think of that she temporarily forgot that she had put Mrs. Cupp's letter in her pocket, and was half-way across the moor before she remembered it.

"Dear me!" she exclaimed when she recalled it. "I must see what has happened."

She opened the envelope and began to read as she walked; but she had not taken many steps before she uttered an exclamation and stopped.

"How very nice for them!" she said, but she turned rather pale.

From a worldly point of view the news the letter contained was indeed very nice for the Cupps, but it put a painful aspect upon the simple affairs of poor Miss Fox-Seton.

"It is a great piece of news, in one way," wrote Mrs. Cupp, "and yet me and Jane can't help feeling a bit low at the thought of the changes it will make, and us living where you won't be with us, if I may take the liberty, miss. My brother William made a good bit of money in Australia, but he has always been homesick for the old country, as he always calls England. His wife was a Colonial, and when she died a year ago he made up his mind to come home to settle in Chichester, where he was born. He says there's nothing like the feeling of a Cathedral town. He's bought such a nice house a bit out, with a big garden, and he wants me and Jane to come and make a home with him. He says he has worked hard all his life, and now he means to be comfortable, and he can't be bothered with housekeeping. He promises to provide well for us both, and he wants us to sell up Mortimer Street, and come as quick as possible. But we *shall* miss you, miss, and though her Uncle William keeps a trap and everything according, and Jane is grateful for his kindness, she broke down and cried hard last night, and says to me: 'Oh, mother, if Miss Fox-Seton could just manage to take me as a maid, I would rather be it than anything. Traps don't feed the heart, mother, and I've a feeling for Miss Fox-Seton as is perhaps unbecoming to my station.' But we've got the men in the house ticketing things, miss, and we want to know what we shall do with the articles in your bed-sitting-room."

The friendliness of the two faithful Cupps and the humble Turkey-red comforts of the bed-sitting-room had meant home to Emily Fox-Seton. When she had turned her face and her tired feet away from discouraging errands and small humiliations and discomforts, she had turned them toward the bed-sitting-room, the hot little fire, the small, fat black kettle singing on the hob, and the two-and-eleven-penny tea-set. Not being given to crossing bridges before she reached them, she had never contemplated the dreary possibility that her refuge might be taken away from her. She had not dwelt upon the fact that she had no other real refuge on earth.

As she walked among the sun-heated heather and the luxuriously droning bees, she dwelt upon it now with a suddenly realising sense. As it came home to her soul, her eyes filled with big tears, which brimmed over and rolled down her cheeks. They dropped upon the breast of her linen blouse and left marks.

"I shall have to find a new bed-sitting-room somewhere," she said, the breast of the linen blouse lifting itself sharply. "It will be so different to be in a house with strangers. Mrs. Cupp and Jane—" She was obliged to take out her handkerchief at that moment. "I am afraid I can't get anything respectable for ten shillings a week. It was very cheap—and they were so nice!"

All her fatigue of the early morning had returned. Her feet began to burn and ache, and the sun felt almost unbearably hot. The mist in her eyes prevented her seeing the path before her. Once or twice she stumbled over something.

"It seems as if it must be farther than four miles," she said. "And then there is the walk back. I *am* tired. But I must get on, really."

Chapter Six

T he drive to the ruins had been a great success. It was a drive of just sufficient length to put people in spirits without fatiguing them. The party came back to lunch with delightful appetites. Lady Agatha and Miss Cora Brooke had pink cheeks. The Marquis of Walderhurst had behaved charmingly to both of them. He had helped each of them to climb about among the ruins, and had taken them both up the steep, dark stairway of one of the towers, and stood with them looking over the turrets into the courtyard and the moat. He knew the history of the castle and could point out the banquet-hall and the chapel and the serving-places, and knew legends about the dungeons.

"He gives us all a turn, mother," said Miss Cora Brooke. "He even gave a turn yesterday to poor Emily Fox-Seton. He's rather nice."

There was a great deal of laughter at lunch after their return. Miss Cora Brooke was quite brilliant in her gay little sallies. But though she was more talkative than Lady Agatha, she did not look more brilliant.

The letter from Curzon Street had not made the beauty shed tears. Her face had fallen when it had been handed to her on her return, and she had taken it upstairs to her room with rather a flagging step. But when she came down to lunch she walked with the movement of a nymph. Her lovely little face wore a sort of tremulous radiance. She laughed like a child at every amusing thing that was said. She might have been ten years old instead of twenty-two, her colour, her eyes, her spirits seemed of a freshness so infantine.

She was leaning back in her chair laughing enchantingly at one of Miss Brooke's sparkling remarks when Lord Walderhurst, who sat next to her, said suddenly, glancing round the table:

"But where is Miss Fox-Seton?"

It was perhaps a significant fact that up to this moment nobody had observed her absence. It was Lady Maria who replied.

"I am almost ashamed to answer," she said. "As I have said before, Emily Fox-Seton has become the lodestar of my existence. I cannot live without her. She has walked over to Maundell to make sure that we do not have a dinner-party without fish to-night."

"She has *walked* over to Maundell," said Lord Walderhurst—"after yesterday?"

"There was not a pair of wheels left in the stable," answered Lady Maria. "It is disgraceful, of course, but she is a splendid walker, and she said she was not too tired to do it. It is the kind of thing she ought to be given the Victoria Cross for—saving one from a dinner-party without fish."

The Marquis of Walderhurst took up the cord of his monocle and fixed the glass rigidly in his eye.

"It is not only four miles to Maundell," he remarked, staring at the table-cloth, not at Lady Maria, "but it is four miles back."

"By a singular coincidence," said Lady Maria.

The talk and laughter went on, and the lunch also, but Lord Walderhurst, for some reason best known to himself, did not finish his. For a few seconds he stared at the table-cloth, then he pushed aside his nearly disposed-of cutlet, then he got up from his chair quietly.

"Excuse me, Maria," he said, and without further ado went out of the room, and walked toward the stables.

There was excellent fish at Maundell; Batch produced it at once, fresh, sound, and desirable. Had she been in her normal spirits, Emily would have rejoiced at the sight of it, and have retraced her four miles to Mallowe in absolute jubilation. She would have shortened and beguiled her return journey by depicting to herself Lady Maria's pleasure and relief.

But the letter from Mrs. Cupp lay like a weight of lead in her pocket. It had given her such things to think of as she walked that she had been oblivious to heather and bees and fleece-bedecked summer-blue sky, and had felt more tired than in any tramp through London streets that she could call to mind. Each step she took seemed to be carrying her farther away from the few square yards of home the bed-sitting-room had represented under the dominion of the Cupps. Every moment she recalled more strongly that it had been home—home. Of course it had not been the third-floor back room so much as it had been the Cupps who made it so, who had regarded her as a sort of possession, who had liked to serve her, and had done it with actual affection.

"I shall have to find a new place," she kept saying. "I shall have to go among quite strange people."

She had suddenly a new sense of being without resource. That was one of the proofs of the curious heaviness of the blow the simple occurrence was to her. She felt temporarily almost as if there were no other lodging-houses in London, though she knew that really there were tens of thousands. The fact was that though there might be other Cupps, or their counterparts, she could not make herself believe such a good thing possible. She had been physically worn out before she had read the letter, and its effect had been proportionate to her fatigue and lack of power to rebound. She was vaguely surprised to feel that the tears kept filling her eyes and falling on her cheeks in big heavy drops. She was obliged to use her handkerchief frequently, as if she was suddenly developing a cold in her head.

"I must take care," she said once, quite prosaically, but with more pathos in her voice than she was aware of, "or I shall make my nose quite red."

The Marquis of Walderhurst

Though Batch was able to supply fish, he was unfortunately not able to send it to Mallowe. His cart had gone out on a round just before Miss Fox-Seton's arrival, and there was no knowing when it would return.

"Then I must carry the fish myself," said Emily. "You can put it in a neat basket."

"I'm very sorry, miss; I am, indeed, miss," said Batch, looking hot and pained.

"It will not be heavy," returned Emily; "and her ladyship must be sure of it for the dinner-party."

So she turned back to recross the moor with a basket of fish on her arm. And she was so pathetically unhappy that she felt that so long as she lived the odour of fresh fish would make her feel sorrowful. She had heard of people who were made sorrowful by the odour of a flower or the sound of a melody but in her case it would be the smell of fresh fish that would make her sad. If she had been a person with a sense of humour, she might have seen that this was thing to laugh at a little. But she was not a humorous woman, and just now—

"Oh, I shall have to find a new place," she was thinking, "and I have lived in that little room for years."

The sun got hotter and hotter, and her feet became so tired that she could scarcely drag one of them after another. She had forgotten that she had left Mallowe before lunch, and that she ought to have got a cup of tea, at least, at Maundell. Before she had walked a mile on her way back, she realised that she was frightfully hungry and rather faint.

"There is not even a cottage where I could get a glass of water," she thought.

The basket, which was really comparatively light, began to feel heavy on her arm, and at length she felt sure that a certain burning spot on her left heel must be a blister which was being rubbed by her shoe. How it hurt her, and how tired she was—how tired! And when she left Mallowe—lovely, luxurious Mallowe—she would not go back to her little room all fresh from the Cupps' autumn house-cleaning, which included the washing and ironing of her Turkey-red hangings and chair-covers; she would be obliged to huddle into any poor place she could find. And Mrs. Cupp and Jane would be in Chichester.

"But what good fortune it is for them!" she murmured. "They need never be anxious about the future again. How—how wonderful it must be to know that one need not be afraid of the future! I—indeed, I think I really must sit down."

She sat down upon the sun-warmed heather and actually let her tear-wet face drop upon her hands.

"Oh, dear! Oh, dear! Oh, dear!" she said helplessly. "I must not let myself do this. I mustn't, Oh, dear! Oh, dear! Oh, dear!"

She was so overpowered by her sense of her own weakness that she was conscious of nothing but the fact that she must control it. Upon the elastic moorland road wheels stole upon one without sound. So the wheels of a rapidly driven high cart approached her and were almost at her side before she lifted her head, startled by a sudden consciousness that a vehicle was near her.

It was Lord Walderhurst's cart, and even as she gazed at him with alarmed wet eyes, his lordship descended from it and made a sign to his groom, who at once impassively drove on.

Emily's lips tried to tremble into a smile; she put out her hand fumblingly toward the fish-basket, and having secured it, began to rise.

"I—sat down to rest," she faltered, even apologetically. "I walked to Maundell, and it was so hot."

Just at that moment a little breeze sprang up and swept across her cheek. She was so grateful that her smile became less difficult.

"I got what Lady Maria wanted," she added, and the childlike dimple in her cheek endeavoured to defy her eyes.

The Marquis of Walderhurst looked rather odd. Emily had never seen him look like this before. He took a silver flask out of his pocket in a matter-of-fact way, and filled its cup with something.

"That is sherry," he said. "Please drink it. You are absolutely faint."

She held out her hand eagerly. She could not help it.

"Oh, thank you—thank you!" she said. "I am *so* thirsty!" And she drank it as if it were the nectar of the gods.

"Now, Miss Fox-Seton," he said, "please sit down again. I came here to drive you back to Mallowe, and the cart will not come back for a quarter of an hour."

"You came on purpose!" she exclaimed, feeling, in truth, somewhat awe-struck. "But how kind of you, Lord Walderhurst—how good!"

It was the most unforeseen and amazing experience of her life, and at once she sought for some reason which could connect with his coming some more interesting person than mere Emily Fox-Seton. Oh,—the thought flashed upon her,—he had come for some reason connected with Lady Agatha. He made her sit down on the heather again, and he took a seat beside her. He looked straight into her eyes.

"You have been crying," he remarked.

There was no use denying it. And what was there in the good gray-brown eye, gazing through the monocle, which so moved her by its suggestion of kindness and—and some new feeling?

"Yes, I have," she admitted. "I don't often—but—well, yes, I have."

"What was it?"

It was the most extraordinary thump her heart gave at this moment. She had never felt such an absolute thump. It was perhaps because she was tired. His voice had lowered itself. No man had ever spoken to her before like that. It made one feel as if he was not an exalted person at all; only a kind, kind one. She must not presume upon his kindness and make much of her prosaic troubles. She tried to smile in a proper casual way.

"Oh, it was a small thing, really," was her effort at treating the matter lightly; "but it seems more important to me than it would to any one with—with a family. The people I live with—who have been so kind to me—are going away."

"The Cupps?" he asked.

She turned quite round to look at him.

"How," she faltered, "did you know about them?"

"Maria told me," he answered, "I asked her."

It seemed such a human sort of interest to have taken in her. She could not understand. And she had thought he scarcely realised her existence. She said to herself that was so often the case—people were so much kinder than one knew.

She felt the moisture welling in her eyes, and stared steadily at the heather, trying to wink it away.

"I am really glad," she explained hastily. "It is such good fortune for them. Mrs. Cupp's brother has offered them such a nice home. They need never be anxious again."

"But they will leave Mortimer Street—and you will have to give up your room."

"Yes. I must find another." A big drop got the better of her, and flashed on its way down her cheek. "I can find a room, perhaps, but—I can't find—" She was obliged to clear her throat.

"That was why you cried?"

"Yes." After which she sat still.

"You don't know where you will live?"

"No."

She was looking so straight before her and trying so hard to behave discreetly that she did not see that he had drawn nearer to her. But a moment later she realised it, because he took hold of her hand. His own closed over it firmly.

"Will you," he said—"I came here, in fact, to ask you if you will come and live with me?"

Her heart stood still, quite still. London was so full of ugly stories about things done by men of his rank—stories of transgressions, of follies, of cruelties. So many were open secrets. There were men, who, even while keeping up an outward aspect of respectability, were held accountable for painful things. The lives of well-born struggling women were so hard. Sometimes such nice ones went under because temptation was so great. But she had not thought, she could not have dreamed—

She got on her feet and stood upright before him. He rose with her, and because she was a tall woman their eyes were on a level. Her own big and honest ones were wide and full of crystal tears.

"Oh!" she said in helpless woe. "Oh!"

It was perhaps the most effective thing a woman ever did. It was so simple that it was heartbreaking. She could not have uttered a word, he was such a powerful and great person, and she was so without help or stay.

Since the occurring of this incident, she has often been spoken of as a beauty, and she has, without doubt, had her fine hours; but Walderhurst has never told her that the most beautiful moment of her life was undoubtedly that in which she stood upon the heather, tall and straight and simple, her hands hanging by her sides, her large, tear-filled hazel eyes gazing straight into his. In the femininity of her frank defencelessness there was an appeal to nature's self in man which was not quite of earth. And for several seconds they stood so and gazed into each other's souls—the usually unilluminated nobleman and the prosaic young woman who lodged on a third floor back in Mortimer Street.

Then, quite quickly, something was lighted in his eyes, and he took a step toward her.

"Good heavens!" he demanded. "What do you suppose I am asking of you?"

"I don't—know," she answered; "I don't—know."

"My good girl," he said, even with some irritation, "I am asking you to be my wife. I am asking you to come and live with me in an entirely respectable manner, as the Marchioness of Walderhurst."

Emily touched the breast of her brown linen blouse with the tips of her fingers.

"You—are—asking—*me*?" she said.

"Yes," he answered. His glass had dropped out of his eye, and he picked it up and replaced it. "There is

Black with the cart," he said. "I will explain myself with greater clearness as we drive back to Mallowe."

The basket of fish was put in the cart, and Emily Fox-Seton was put in. Then the marquis got in himself, and took the reins from his groom.

"You will walk back, Black," he said, "by that path," with a wave of the hand in a diverging direction.

As they drove across the heather, Emily was trembling softly from head to foot. She could have told no human being what she felt. Only a woman who had lived as she had lived and who had been trained as she had been trained could have felt it. The brilliance of the thing which had happened to her was so unheard of and so undeserved, she told herself. It was so incredible that, even with the splendid gray mare's high-held head before her and Lord Walderhurst by her side, she felt that she was only part of a dream. Men had never said "things" to her, and a man was saying them—the Marquis of Walderhurst was saying them. They were not the kind of things every man says or said in every man's way, but they so moved her soul that she quaked with joy.

"I am not a marrying man," said his lordship, "but I must marry, and I like you better than any woman I have ever known. I do not generally like women. I am a selfish man, and I want an unselfish woman. Most women are as selfish as I am myself. I used to like you when I heard Maria speak of you. I have watched you and thought of you ever since I came here. You are necessary to everyone, and you are so modest that you know nothing about it. You are a handsome woman, and you are always thinking of other women's good looks."

Emily gave a soft little gasp.

"But Lady Agatha," she said. "I was sure it was Lady Agatha."

"I don't want a girl," returned his lordship. "A girl would bore me to death. I am not going to dry-nurse a girl at the age of fifty-four. I want a companion."

"But I am so *far* from clever," faltered Emily.

The marquis turned in his driving-seat to look at her. It was really a very nice look he gave her. It made Emily's cheeks grow pink and her simple heart beat.

"You are the woman I want," he said. "You make me feel quite sentimental."

When they reached Mallowe, Emily had upon her finger the ruby which Lady Maria had graphically described as being "as big as a trouser button." It was, indeed, so big that she could scarcely wear her glove over it. She was still incredible, but she was blooming like a large rose. Lord Walderhurst had said so many "things" to her that she seemed to behold a new heaven and a new earth. She had been so swept off her feet that she had not really been allowed time to think, after that first gasp, of Lady Agatha.

When she reached her bedroom she almost returned to earth as she remembered it. Neither of them had dreamed of this—neither of them. What could she say to Lady Agatha? What would Lady Agatha say to her, though it had not been her fault? She had not dreamed that such a thing could be possible. How could she, oh, how could she?

She was standing in the middle of her room with clasped hands. There was a knock upon the door, and Lady Agatha herself came to her.

What had occurred? Something. It was to be seen in the girl's eyes, and in a certain delicate shyness in her manner.

"Something very nice has happened," she said.

"Something nice?" repeated Emily.

Lady Agatha sat down. The letter from Curzon Street was in her hand half unfolded.

"I have had a letter from mamma. It seems almost bad taste to speak of it so soon, but we have talked to each other so much, and you are so kind, that I want to tell you myself. Sir Bruce Norman has been to talk to papa about—about me."

Emily felt that her cup filled to the brim at the moment.

"He is in England again?"

Agatha nodded gently.

"He only went away to—well, to test his own feelings before he spoke. Mamma is delighted with him. I am going home to-morrow."

Emily made a little swoop forward.

"You always liked him?" she said.

Lady Agatha's delicate mounting colour was adorable.

"I was quite *unhappy*," she owned, and hid her lovely face in her hands.

In the morning-room Lord Walderhurst was talking to Lady Maria.

"You need not give Emily Fox-Seton any more clothes, Maria," he said. "I am going to supply her in future. I have asked her to marry me."

Lady Maria lightly gasped, and then began to laugh.

"Well, James," she said, "you have certainly much more sense than most men of your rank and age."

CPSIA information can be obtained at www.ICGtesting.com
Printed in the USA
LVOW06s2247130214

373674LV00001B/310/P